222 Pages

THE

LAZARUS LONGMAN
CHRONICLES

ONE
DIME

SILVER TOMB

P. J. Thorndyke

LONDON

Number 2   1886

Silver Tomb
By P. J. Thorndyke

2015 by Copyright © P. J. Thorndyke

Contents

CHAPTER ONE

In which our hero is unperturbed by the sound of an exploding horse

As the voices of the muezzins from their minarets carried across the rooftops of the city calling all Mohammedans to *Asr*—the third of the five daily prayers—the heat of the day had barely relented. In his room on the third floor of Shepheard's Hotel, Lazarus Longman listened to the sounds of the Cairo afternoon while he dragged a straight razor across his cheeks and neck, scraping off a mixture of sweat, black bristles and Vinolia Shaving Soap. He carefully avoided the bristles on his top lip, leaving his very neat and very English looking moustache untouched.

He halted as the sound of the explosion echoed down the street below his window and up the walls of the buildings, sending a startled flock of hooded crows flapping and cawing from the roof of a nearby mosque. He held the straight razor frozen an inch from his cheek during the stunned silence that followed the deafening roar, and when the cries of alarm quickly filled the vacuum, he resumed shaving, as uninterested

1

in the racket as he was unsurprised.

He had seen the fools trying to get the iron horse in motion on his way back to the hotel that afternoon. Several *fellahs* had put it into service pulling a cartload of dates. No matter how backward, every country on the globe was trying to imitate the technological leaps and bounds that had been reported and remarked upon in the Confederate and United States of America; a land Lazarus had spent a good deal of time in over the past year. It was true that the streets of American cities were stalked by the iron hooves of steam-powered beasts of burden. Cabs were drawn by remarkable metal contraptions on four legs, belching steam and clanking along with the stuttering and jarring one might expect from a stiff corpse brought back from the dead.

But these were mere pedestrian toys in comparison to the terrifying war machines that continent had dreamed up and put into action in its twenty-five-year-long war. And the countries outside its borders, try as they might, would never even perfect a mechanical donkey without access to the valuable ore known as mechanite which seemed to be unique to the North American continent.

That didn't stop the construction of damn-fool contraptions like the one that had just exploded near Shepheard's Hotel. In the absence of mechanite, the idiots had over-fuelled the coal furnace and let the steam build up to an irresponsible level, resulting in the inevitable explosion. Lazarus had seen this and had tried to warn them, but the fellahs in charge of the contraption had taken his protest as yet another English interference in the Egyptian's natural drive for advancement and had shouted him away. The contraption was a sorry, slapdash affair that would likely have come apart at the rivets before long anyway. They had even put a daft head with ears on the thing that looked like an ironmonger had tried to make a hobby horse for a pantomime.

After his warning had been ignored and he had been rudely ushered on his way, Lazarus had shrugged his shoulders and gone up to the hotel to dress for dinner. He didn't allow his sense of satisfaction at the sound of the mechanical horse exploding draw a smile on his lips. It was bloody dangerous to let simple farmers tinker around with coal furnaces and steam. He didn't doubt that more than one of the fellahs had been scalded in the incident.

He finished shaving and wiped away the residue with a cloth before fixing a collar to his shirt. He went over to the armchair where the morning edition of the *Egyptian Gazette* lay; one of dozens of newspapers printed to cater to the country's large English-speaking population.

He picked it up and rifled through it for the second time that afternoon. There was a report on the continuing investigation into the murder of a renowned Egyptologist whose body had been found scorched and mutilated down at the Bulaq docks. But the main story was the approaching visit of the *CSS Scorpion II*; the gigantic Confederate airship that, stripped of its guns, was crossing the Atlantic and making its way for Cairo on what was, for all Lazarus could gather, a mere show of might.

He scanned the article once more with distaste. The interest of the Confederate States in Egypt and the Suez Canal was worrying. Officially Britain and the C.S.A. were allies, but this landing of the airship in Cairo had the Khedive dancing with glee at the prospect of his British overlord's humiliation. The inevitable overshadowing of their technological and military might by their American cousins, as well as the promise of further foreign investment in his country's fledgling economy would be pleasing to him indeed. The British had held Egypt in a vice of colonialism – however unofficially – ever since they had helped him wrangle the Khedivate back from the nationalist faction of the army and had since showed no signs of loosening their grip.

Now that Her Majesty's empire had its hand in the running of Egypt's economy, it would not take kindly to any American interference in its domination of the trade routes with India. Egypt was not officially part of the empire, but Britain had a financial investment in the improving economy of the country, and had appointed Evelyn Baring, the first Earl of Cromer, as their liaison with the new Khedive.

But allies or not, Lazarus Longman hated the Confederacy with a passion. It had been a gift of fortune that he had escaped from that blasted collection of states with his life, and nothing short of a miracle that he still had a job within the bureau after the debacle of the golden cities of Cibola. But he had bluffed his way through the endless debriefings, bending the truth at times and outright lying at others, and somehow had come out of it unscathed. Now, a year later, he had a different assignment.

Morton had explained the situation to him in his office at Whitehall. He had poured cognac from a decanter into two glasses, muttering irritably as he splashed a fleck on a nearby stack of paperwork.

"It's a missing person's job," Morton said, easing himself down into his chair.

"A bit pedestrian for your office, isn't it?" Lazarus asked. "Why not let the police handle it?"

"It's in Egypt."

"Then why not let the Egyptian police handle it? The consul has his own special branch there, yes?"

"The Mamur Zapt? Yes, well, it's a little more complicated than that. And I want you specifically to handle it. The case is made for you, or so it seems."

"Oh?"

"You know the party involved, you see."

"Has somebody I know gone missing? I really must keep a closer eye on my acquaintances."

"It's not the missing one you know, but her fiancé."

"Who?"

"Henry Thackeray."

"That pompous arse? Why on earth would I care about his love life, much as it surprises me that he has one."

Morton leveled his eyes at him. "You are not required to *care* about any case beyond your sense of duty to Her Majesty."

"Oh, well played, that, man," Lazarus said in a withering tone. "The old 'duty to the crown' card. It's been at least a year since you used that one on me."

Morton sighed and set down his glass, leaning forward as if the conversation required a more intimate touch. "Look, I know the past few years have been a bloody bad show for you, Longman. I don't blame you if your confidence in the bureau has been shaken. First that bad business in Colombia and then the Cibola washout; it's been a rotten spot of luck. But this affair should be simple enough. A quick job to get you back on your feet, as it were. And your acquaintance with Thackeray isn't the only reason I chose you for the job."

"No? You mean you're handing me this routine plod case because you don't trust me with anything bigger?"

"Not at all. It's Egypt, man! Your area of expertise."

"I have many areas of expertise. Got the diplomas to prove it."

"Among which Egyptology ranks in the first class."

"Tell me, Morton," Lazarus said, "does this missing persons case call much for the reading of hieroglyphics? The ability to place every known pharaoh in his correct dynasty?"

Morton frowned. "Of course not. But you know Cairo. You know the Nile. You probably know every seedy tavern and shady spot better than I dare to guess. And that is what makes you our prime candidate for the job."

"You still haven't said what the job is other than it has something to do with some blower Thackeray has misplaced."

"It's not some blower. Its Eleanor Rousseau, one of France's leading Egyptologists."

Morton had Lazarus's attention now. "I've heard of her. She was one of Mariette's brightest disciples. Knows hieroglyphics better than Champollion did. Thackeray was running around with *her*?"

"Until she went missing. Ordinarily we wouldn't care a fig for a French Egyptologist but it's her relationship with Thackeray that has us worried not to mention the reasons for her sudden disappearing act. He shouldn't have been running around with a French woman, not a man in his position, considering Britain's relationship with France."

"Yes, I hear he's been appointed to the House of

6

Lords."

"Indeed. And his relationship with a French woman was strongly discouraged by the PM and kept hidden from Her Majesty."

"Why on earth did they give him a seat?"

"Lord knows. He's a powerful man and has the type of connections that makes a lowly civil servant like me positively green."

Lazarus smirked. Morton was anything but a 'lowly civil servant' and had connections of his own that were enough to give any man a case of the willies. But still, since Henry Thackeray had come into his inheritance, he was a force to be reckoned with in political circles.

"Whitehall's worried that this French slip of his knows far too much and her disappearance has them in a funk. There are even concerns that she may have maintained a relationship with Thackeray merely to get information from him."

"You mean they think she's a spy?"

"That's one concern."

"An Egyptologist? Funny sort of training for a career as a secret agent…" and then he caught himself. His own career matched that statement exactly and they both knew it. "So, what's the Egyptian connection?"

"That's where she's resurfaced."

"If you know where she is then why am I here?"

"We don't know exactly where in Egypt she is. Her name has come up in Cairo a couple of times and then nothing. It's likely she's out on some dig in the desert. I don't suppose that during your travels in the C.S.A. you ever came across the name Rutherford Lindholm?"

Lazarus shook his head.

"He's an American. From Virginia. A brilliant scientist in the areas of neurology, galvanism and something called 'bio-mechanics'."

As soon as he heard the word Lazarus felt a deep feeling of unease. "Bio-mechanics?"

"Yes. It's all to do with those ghastly mechanical slaves they build over there. The fusion of the biological with the mechanical. You yourself encountered some of his creations during your time on that continent."

Lazarus suppressed a shudder when he thought of the Mecha-warriors, Mecha-whores and other monstrosities he had witnessed in the Confederate States. He also thought of Hok'ee, or Pahanatuuwa to use his birth name; that gigantic native who had suffered horrific mutilations at the hands of Confederate scientists in their pursuit to perfect a warrior—part man, part machine.

"Professor Lindholm was one of the pioneers of the mechanite revolution, specifically in the creation of mechanical-men. They have organic pilots, you know of course, plugged into steam-powered suits with mechanite furnaces. Bloody unchristian, if you ask me."

"So what does this Lindholm have to do with Eleanor Rousseau?"

"I'm getting to that. It seems that Lindholm has run into difficulties in his homeland. Some sort of legal bother. He's gone rogue, fleeing America and popping up suddenly in Egypt."

"Where he met Rousseau."

"Exactly."

"But why?"

"That's what we want you to find out. Now the

C.S.A. are our friends, politically speaking, so ordinarily we wouldn't touch him. But if he's gone rogue…"

"Then we can grab him and squeeze him for secrets. I just don't see the Rousseau connection."

"Neither do we, but they've been seen together, and she has written to her fiancé—ex- fiancé, I should imagine by now—that she was embarking on a dig with an eminent American scientist, although she didn't mention his name. We don't know what his interest in Egyptology is, and quite frankly the whole business has us stumped. Shortly after Rousseau's letter to Thackeray, all correspondence stopped. He even went over there to find her, but all traces of her have vanished. He's worried that she may be romantically involved with Lindholm."

Lazarus snorted with mirth.

"The poor bugger's frantic. Reuniting the two isn't in our interests of course but bringing her back to Blighty is top priority. National safety aside, it could avoid a very nasty scandal; House of Lords member bedding a French spy, that sort of thing. And the more you find out about this Lindholm, the better. It's probably just a nasty bit of sordidness, you know how these French are. Still, worth a look."

Chapter Two

**In which some excellent tobacco and coffee is
had despite the less than savory surroundings**

Lazarus left the hotel and tilted his bowler hat
to shield his eyes from the sun reflecting off
the pale sandstone walls of the buildings. It
would soon be dark and the great god in the sky was
giving a last, heroic fight before he would be swallowed
by the night, as if the same battle had not been fought
and lost every day since the dawn of time.

The remains of the iron horse still smoldered in the
street as the fellahs doused it with cold water. The
steam rose up in billows from its split boiler, and two
of them were receiving medical attention from a
passerby. Lazarus ignored them and followed the
railings of Azbekya Gardens through which he could
see the opera house, partially screened by tamarisks
and carob trees. He headed towards the Grand
Continental Hotel.

When he had arrived in Cairo he had only one lead,
and that lead was a man. Flinders Petrie. Lazarus had
run into England's preeminent Egyptologist in
eighteen-eighty when he had been working for the
Royal Archeological Society. Petrie had been the first
man to make an accurate survey of the pyramids at
Gizah. The two of them had taken to each other
instantly.

He found Petrie in the foyer of the Grand Continental Hotel, dressed for dinner. He was about the same age as Lazarus; thin with a long, bearded face and thick black hair.

"Good lord, Longman!" Petrie said, extending his hand. "To think we should meet in Cairo once again! How on earth are you?"

"As well as can be expected, Flinders!" said Lazarus, shaking Petrie's hand vigorously. "Still yearning for the days when the biggest worry was running out of funds or being robbed by our Berber guides!"

"Yes, I understand you work for the government now. And you've been in America! You must tell me about it."

"Over dinner, perhaps. Where shall we go? The food at Shepheard's is awful. How is it here?"

"Worse. But you must remember that little restaurant on the other side of the gardens? The one with the waiter with the glass eye?"

"Good lord, I'd forgotten!"

They ignored the shoeshine boys who chased after them with blackened brushes as they made their way towards the restaurant. Aside from the hanging plants and slowly rotating fans, the interior of the restaurant could have been seen anywhere in London or Paris. Rows of dark wooden seating booths lined the oblong dining room and the tables were spread with white linen embroidered in arabesque designs. They sat down and ordered. Petrie had ham in champagne sauce and Lazarus ordered a plate of breaded calf's tongues with a bottle of Chateau Rautzan.

"What new things have you been digging up then, Flinders?" Lazarus asked his companion. "Last I heard you were at Tell Nebesheh."

"Oh yes. We found some fantastic tombs filled with statuettes and a wonderful royal sphinx from the twelfth dynasty."

Lazarus smiled at his use of the term 'we'. Petrie was known for rolling his shirt sleeves up and pitching in with the laborers in his pursuit of artifacts, dispensing with foremen entirely, something which set him apart from his peers in that field. He also insisted on paying out rewards for items found, ensuring that they were handled with care and not stolen. It also ensured that Petrie was ever desperately short of funds.

"More recently I have been at a dig at Tell el-Amarna. There's some fascinating building work from the eighteenth dynasty beneath all the Roman and Christian layers. We found a beautiful painted pavement showing all kinds of daily life, worth its weight in gold, although Maspero and all the others don't see it. I seem to be the only Egyptologist in Egypt who believes that we can learn more about the past from bits of broken pottery than we can from all the sensational finds."

"How is the new director of the Department of Antiquities working out?" Lazarus asked. In the six years since he had left Egypt, the esteemed Auguste Mariette had died and been replaced by Gaston Maspero.

"Oh, he's not so bad," Petrie replied. "A little chaotic, but his heart is in the right place. He's dedicated to preserving the antiquities and sites of Egypt and brought big improvements on the treasure hunting practices of the old days. He's a shrewd businessman too, letting certain artifacts slip out of the country for favors. Not that he's corrupt, mind you. He comes down hard on the antiquities black market whenever he has a chance, which shows that he's not only interested in the monetary value of things. Do you know he's proposing admission charges for tourists wishing to visit ancient sites? It's part of his plan to pay for their upkeep. Not a bad idea at all. And he's currently engaged in uncovering the rest of the Sphinx at Gizah. He's convinced there are tombs down there, as am I. The next few months will be terribly exciting if he can shift all that sand."

"Indeed. But Tell el-Amarna, that's the city Akhenaten built, isn't it?"

"Yes, the Heretic Pharaoh. A fascinating place. I have a number of interesting artifacts I found there if you'd like to take a look. Except two of them have been stolen, curse it."

"Stolen?"

"Yes. There was a theft at the Bulaq Museum the other week. A relief fragment was pinched right under Maspero's nose. I was the one who found it, and it was a priceless example of the distinctive artistic style of Akhenaten's reign. Now it's gone. Also, I lost a cosmetic box I dug up at Tell el-Amarna. But that crime is overshadowed of course by the grisly murder of its custodian."

"Really? I read about that in the paper. Did you know the fellow?"

"Yes, he was a friend of mine."

"I'm sorry."

"I lent him the artifact the day before. I can't help but accept some of the blame for his death. Had I not lent him the item, perhaps he would never have attracted the attention of a murdering thug."

"And they've had no luck in finding the killer? The papers are hopelessly in the dark."

"As are the police. He was found with his neck broken and his hands and forearms terribly scorched, as if he had placed them upon a hotplate."

"Most strange."

They finished eating and Petrie sat swirling his claret around in his glass expectantly. He had been very patient, Lazarus gave him that. But now he could wait no more. "I've told you enough about my activities since we last saw each other, Longman. Now I think it's time you told me yours. Why have you returned to Egypt? What business has Her Majesty's government got you on?"

"You've caught me out, Petrie," said Lazarus with a smile. "It's been wonderful seeing you again but you're absolutely right in thinking that my meeting you is more than a wish to catch up with an old friend. I need to ask you a question. Have you ever met Mademoiselle Eleanor Rousseau?"

"No," Petrie replied. "But I sorely wish I had. She's very highly respected in my field. For a woman that is. She's the one who discovered Akhenaten's tomb in the Valley of the Kings last year. A wonderful find."

"Odd that your paths have never crossed, with both of you being here in Egypt."

"Not really. I spend so much time out at digs that I rarely come into Cairo. In fact, it was lucky that I was at the hotel when you called. As for Rousseau, she's even harder to find. She's rarely in Cairo at all, by all accounts. Virtually lives out on some dig somewhere with an American fellow."

"Ah, so you've heard of him too."

"Lindholm or something or other. Haven't heard much about his reputation as an Egyptologist at all. Probably just another treasure hunter, as if Egypt

15

needed any more. But I would be very disappointed if Mademoiselle Rousseau was helping him in any way to rob this land of its cultural riches."

"Are they courting?"

"How should I know, Longman? I've met neither and care little for the sordid affairs of others. Is this really why the government sent you out here?"

"Rousseau is the fiancé of Henry Thackeray."

"Good lord, really? The fellow you had that very public spat with a few years ago?"

"That's the one."

"Well I'm surprised you are doing him a favor after the things he said about you in the *London Illustrated.*"

"Lord, no. My orders are to find Rousseau and get her back to England. Whitehall thinks she's some sort of spy and is worried about what she knows. Any sordidness is not really my problem. Now, Flinders, tell me what you know."

Flinders looked around at the other patrons in the restaurant. "Very well, but here might not be the wisest place to discuss certain things."

"What do you mean?"

"I mean that there are aspects of Mademoiselle Rousseau's activities here in Egypt that have aroused the attention of organizations, like the police."

Lazarus was intrigued. Finally his mission seemed to be turning out to be something a little more exciting than a missing persons case. "All right. How about I take you to a little place I know for coffee? It's a local establishment and frequented more by natives than the British. Just the place people go to discuss things without being overheard."

"Sounds capital, Longman."

They paid their bill and left the restaurant, heading

north of Azbekya Gardens. The northern part of the city was the decidedly older part, filled with dim alleys and shuttered windows, the darkness behind their lattices concealing things the British authorities were all too happy to believe did not exist. Not all the windows were shuttered. Some opened onto balconies where the city's courtesans leaned, peering down onto the uneven streets, the oil lamps illuminating their curves, barely concealed behind white silk gowns.

The coffee shop was nestled within a row of arches, entirely shaded. The haze of smoke that passed out between the arches came from the hookahs or 'hubble-bubbles'; the water pipes favored by the Egyptians. They took their shoes off and entered, letting their eyes grow accustomed to the light. The ceiling was low, supported by arabesque arches. Groups of men in native dress sat about in small groups on cushions, drinking coffee and smoking.

"By Jove, you know some rum dives!" exclaimed Petrie.

They found an isolated spot and sat down. The proprietor came hurrying over with his coffee jug, from which he poured a steaming black stream into two cups. Lazarus ordered a hookah for them to share.

"They use Turkish tobacco here," Lazarus explained. "Far superior to the local stuff which tastes like burning mummy rags."

"I'll remember that," said Petrie, eyeing the contraption the proprietor had brought over with suspicion.

They drank their coffee and took drags on the hookah, relaxing into the cushions as if they were both born and bred Cairenes.

"You know, this stuff's not half bad," said Petrie,

letting the smoke blast out through his nostrils. "And the coffee is excellent too. You certainly can show me a thing or two about local establishments, Longman."

"I'm glad you like it. And we're the only foreigners in the place."

Petrie looked around. It was true. The locals didn't seem to mind their presence, either.

"Now, if you feel quite safe enough," said Lazarus, "please continue with what you were telling me in the restaurant."

"Right. Last I heard, Rousseau was expanding on my dig at Tell el Amarna. I don't believe there's anything left there to find and I suspect that she found this out, for she has since moved on. Where to, I don't know, but acquaintances of mine who have met her say she's obsessed with Akhenaten and the Amarna period."

Lazarus nodded slowly. Petrie didn't have to fill him in about Akhenaten. Any student of Egyptology knew that particular pharaoh well. Known as the Heretic Pharaoh, Akhenaten had been born Amenhotep IV before he changed his name along with the entire religion of Egypt. His reign marked a sudden shift in the official faith of the land, from its many gods to the worship of a single solar deity represented by the sun, known as the 'Aten'. Akhenaten (meaning 'effective for Aten') moved the royal court from Thebes to a new city he had constructed on the eastern bank of the Nile at Tell el-Amarna, in accordance with the rising sun. This was named Akhetaten, which meant 'horizon of the Aten'.

This early attempt at monotheism did not outlast the life of its greatest proponent, however, and with Akhenaten's death, his queen Nefertiti and the rest of the court moved back to Thebes. Subsequent pharaohs restored Egypt's polytheism and declared Akhenaten a heretic, defacing his statues and razing Akhetaten to the ground. It wasn't until Rousseau discovered his tomb that many of the blanks of his life could be filled in.

"It was around the time of Rousseau's disappearance that certain items began appearing on the black market," Petrie went on. "Items the like of which I have never seen before."

"How so?"

"For instance, Longman, as a fellow Egyptologist, have you ever seen or heard of an ushabti made of solid silver?"

Lazarus shook his head. Ushabtis were the little funerary statuettes found in tombs, made to represent the deceased should they be called upon to do any kind of manual labor in the afterlife. Naturally many ushabtis represented servants to fill in for those wealthy enough to have owned servants in life.

"And how about scarabs?" continued Petrie, "or any other funerary goods for that matter?"

"No," said Lazarus. "Silver wasn't a preferred metal for the Ancient Egyptians, being rarer than gold in this part of the world."

"Yes, they tended to use gold to represent the glory of the gods, especially the Aten, gold being a handy stand-in for the sun's glare. But some of these silver items specifically allude to the Aten, suggesting that there is another aspect to Akhenaten's religion that we have previously been blind to."

"A silver Aten," mused Lazarus. "The moon, perhaps?"

"That was my conclusion as well. A number of

these items have been reported on the black market, and any significance other than their material value is lost on all but the likes of us Egyptologists. Maspero and the Egyptian police have been trying to crack an illegal antiquities ring for years without success, long before these silver items began appearing on the market. The goods are probably brought into the city by fellahs who have some access to the tombs. Maybe they live in their localities and have kept their discoveries secret, or perhaps they are employed as workmen on digs and are hiding items in their breeches, I honestly don't know. What I do know is that some of the items I've seen have come from tombs undiscovered, officially speaking."

"Undiscovered?"

"For example, I have seen with my own eyes a funerary necklace passing hands that bore the cartouche of Ramses II."

"A funerary necklace? But that could only have been buried with the mummy of its owner."

"And the mummy of Ramses II has never been found! Exactly! And there's more—a ring belonging to Seti I and an ushabti bearing Thutmose II's name. The list goes on. We know that it wasn't uncommon for the ancient Egyptians to remove the mummies of their forefathers from tombs threatened by robbers and hide them in other tombs, often several mummies cached together. To me it seems that somebody somewhere knows the location of a cache of royal mummies that may contain every undiscovered pharaoh mentioned on any king list anywhere!"

"And you believe that these silver items come from the same dealers?"

"Well, it seems reasonable to think so. Even if the

source of the silver Aten items is not the same as this royal cache, then the items are following the same channels onto the black market."

"But do you really think Eleanor Rousseau is behind it all? Even if she is the one who has discovered some sort of temple to the silver Aten, it doesn't fit with what I know about her to be selling priceless items to tourists."

"No, I quite agree. But as I said, perhaps the fellahs working on her dig are palming the artifacts without her knowledge. If so, there has to be a great many of them for some to escape her notice."

"But where is this dig?" Lazarus asked.

"Ah, that's the real question, isn't it? Nobody knows. No new concession has been recorded in Lindholm's or Rousseau's name, so if they really have found some new site they're keeping it to themselves. And nobody's seen hide or hair of them for a long time."

"Perhaps they were murdered by their workmen for control of the artifacts."

Petrie frowned as he took another drag of the hookah. "Not unlikely, one fears."

"Either way, I have to find out."

"Well, I've told you all I know and given you my thoughts on the matter. How do you intend to proceed?"

"Right now, the black market is our only possible link to Rousseau," said Lazarus. "And that is the lead we must follow."

Chapter Three

In which a short voyage in the Bulaq Harbor comes to a disastrous end

The night was still young, despite the somber darkness of the streets and the still air whispering through the alleys. In other parts of Cairo, one might still find Europeans sitting on the streets outside cafes, sipping coffee and watching the nightlife saunter past. But north of Azbekya Gardens, doors were bolted, and lamps blown out in windows.

The only life seen in the streets was the scurrying of rats, and the only sounds heard were the occasional hurried footsteps of some citizen on a late errand. There were cafes in this neglected district, but they did not advertise their existence. Only those who knew Cairo's darkest secrets knew where to find these dim cellars where the scent of scalding coffee was often masked by the more pungent odor of hashish.

"Are you sure you know where you're taking me?" Petrie asked, his voice betraying his tingling nerves. It was not a question of geography—he was sure Lazarus knew the city as well as any Cairene—but the darkness in the alleys seemed to be growing all about them as they delved deeper and deeper into this crumbling, seldom visited district. He did not openly challenge his companion's wisdom in this late-night foray into the city's seedy underbelly but hurried to keep up as

Lazarus took one alley after the other, following some map in his head.

"We're quite safe," Lazarus said. "Do you carry a revolver?"

"Certainly not."

"You should, you know."

"I tend to do my damndest to avoid a situation where I might have need of one."

"As do I, but if we want to get to the bottom of this black market business, then we must pursue my only doorway into that world. And that doorway is a man called Murad."

Petrie suppressed a wince at Lazarus's use of the word 'we'. At no point had he expressed a desire to become an accomplice to Lazarus's mission and at no point had Lazarus questioned the idea that he might not want to. But as they dashed down the dusty, nighted streets in pursuit of their lead, Petrie could hardly argue that he was not a little bit excited.

"So who is this Murad and how do you know him?" he panted as they rounded another corner.

"Smuggler. Black market merchant. I had an encounter with him back in eighty-one. That was over some antiquities that had gone missing. But Cromer was interested in him for smuggling more than looted treasures."

"Guns?"

"All manner of weapons that seemed to find their way into the hands of the Mahdi's dervishes, as well as various nationalist groups."

"Is he one of those blighters?"

"No. His pursuit of profit outweighs any political views. And that makes him useful to us."

They finally arrived at their destination. It was a

sorry two-storey building that could have been a house, a shop, a café or all three combined, for its blank walls and dark windows betrayed no secrets. A set of steps led down to a cellar lit by oil lamps from which the sound of many voices could be heard.

Their entrance warranted a lot more scrutiny than their visit to the previous coffee shop had. White men were almost never seen in these places, and if they were, they always spelled trouble. Lazarus nodded at the proprietor who seemed to recall his face and came over. "Coffee please," Lazarus said.

The man nodded and poured them both cups. "You have returned, *Ingleezeh*."

Petrie raised his eyebrows. The lack of the respectful term 'effendi'—often used by native to Englishman—indicated that Lazarus was considered to be on a more equal footing with these Egyptian night owls than the average white man.

"I'm looking for Murad," said Lazarus.

The man seemed a little relieved that there was not more to their visit than the pursuit of antiquities and set the coffee pot down. "He's upstairs. I will get him if you would like to make yourselves comfortable."

They went over to some cushions and sipped their coffee. After a while their man came down the steps from the floor above, fastening his breeches and looking flushed.

"Still haunting this shit-hole, Murad?" Lazarus said to the man.

Murad froze as he saw Lazarus. His eyes darted to the door as if calculating his chances of making it out onto the street before somebody could put their hands on him. He decided they were slim. "*Effendi*! It has been many years! What brings you back to Cairo?"

"Come and sit with us and we'll tell you."

The man threw more nervous glances about and decided that he was safe enough for the time being and sat down.

"I hope you are still in the antiquities business or our trip has been wasted," Lazarus told the man while motioning for more coffee to be brought.

"I… ah… yes," said Murad, not knowing which was the wisest answer to give. "You wish to buy again? I remember you as a very hard bargainer. I'm not sure my purse could take another of your beatings. Daylight robbery, really."

"Luckily for you it's nighttime," Lazarus reminded him. "And this time I'm looking for something extra special. If you don't have it, I'd appreciate your telling me where else I might look."

Murad leaned in closer, his greedy eyes alight at the prospect of a customer's desperation. "What is it this time?"

"Silver items dating from the eighteenth dynasty, particularly from the reign of Akhenaten."

Murad's eyes narrowed and a look of worry creased his brow. "Unheard of," he said.

"*We've* heard of them," said Lazarus. "They would be very new to the market. In the last year or so. They come from a new dig, the whereabouts of which is uncertain."

Murad's face remained grave and he said nothing.

"These are priceless items," Lazarus went on. "They signify an aspect of the Aten worship that we know nothing about. Their value to the antiquarian society far outweighs their material value. Whoever could lead us to them would be rewarded handsomely."

Murad seemed to reconsider his stance. "Ah, the

Aten worship, of course. You must forgive me, sirs, I am not as well educated in my own country's history as you are. Yes, I know a man who has come by some of these items of silver. But he is himself a collector and I do not think he would be willing to part with them for their mere street value."

"Just tell us where we can find him and leave the bargaining to us," Lazarus said.

Murad made a show of looking around the cellar with caution. "He owns a shipping company on the docks. The name is Bayoumi. It's a big place. Ask around and you'll find it but for the love of Allah, don't tell anybody I sent you. The police are making things hard enough for me as it is, and I don't want to endanger my business relationship with Mr. Bayoumi."

"Very well," said Lazarus. "You have been most helpful. Thank you."

Murad nodded and scurried off, having suddenly decided that he was tired and needed no further entertainment for the evening.

The following morning, they found the Bulaq docks more than living up to their reputed state of filth, bustle and decay. Gulls wheeled over the wharves, swooping down to snatch fish from the boats and off the carts taking them to market. Rats scurried along the gutters and up the mooring lines of the *dahabeahs*. It was well known that those spacious vessels were riddled with rats and insects, despite their popularity in previous years with European tourists wishing to venture up the Nile. Since the steamers had begun to churn the waters, the *dahabeah* business had fallen into disrepair along

27

with the majority of their vessels, several of which could be seen rotting at their moorings.

"Lord, I couldn't sleep a wink," said Petrie as he approached Lazarus at their arranged meeting point. He was ten minutes late and looked pale and ill. "Too much bloody coffee for one evening."

Lazarus smiled. Despite the Egyptologist's complaints, he seemed as ready as ever to embark on their second round of detective work. *The excitement of digging holes in the desert and reading in dusty libraries must be wearing thin on the young scholar,* he thought.

They began asking around and were eventually directed to a large building with Arabic lettering painted on one side. Lazarus, whose Arabic was better than Petrie's, read it aloud; "Bayoumi Shipping Inc. or something to that effect."

It was an old building made from sandstone with crumbling and worn edges. Several scarred piers poked out into the harbor like gnarled fingers at which hulking steamers were moored, their sides grimy with rust. Inside the office, they found the manager leaning back in his chair with his feet on the desk as he went through paperwork. He was a fat man with a scarred face.

"Good morning," said Lazarus.

The only parts of the man that moved in response were his eyes as they looked up at them from his papers.

"We are looking to buy one of your company's steamers. Is it possible to speak with Mr. Bayoumi?"

"Steamers not for sale," said the manager.

"We represent a very wealthy businessman, sir," said Lazarus. "And I believe that Mr. Bayoumi would be very interested in talking to us."

The man continued to stare at them as if sizing them up. "Very well." The man's legs came down to rest on the floor, along with the front two legs of his chair. "I shall see if he is available. Wait here please."

They stood around in the pokey office, littered with untidy piles of documentation and smelling of stale coffee and sweat. Once or twice a heavy-set Egyptian came in to add a fresh bundle to the piles, eyeing the two strangers suspiciously. Eventually the manager returned.

"Come with me."

He stood back to let them go through the door first and they proceeded in that awkward stumbling manner one follows when asked to lead the way through their host's property. They wound up on the spacious floor of the warehouse. Several hulls were under repair and piles of crates, sails, timbers and other nautical detritus were piled up all around. Three chairs had been set up in the centre of the room, and other than a large man in a European business suit and a scarlet tarboosh, the place was deserted. Lazarus had caught sight of the last of the workers departing on their way in, refusing to make eye contact with them. He looked at the vacant chairs and at the two thick-set laborers who had suddenly materialized on either side of the manager and decided that he did not like this situation at all.

"Gentlemen," said the big, suited man. "I am Mr. Bayoumi. Please, sit down and I can have some refreshments brought."

Lazarus did not like the idea of sitting down with heavies all about them but saw no polite way to refuse. They sat down. So did Mr. Bayoumi.

"What can I do for you gentlemen?" He was smiling as if he was in on a secret they knew nothing about.

29

"Ahmed tells me that you are interested in buying a boat. I have to say that I do not usually sell my vessels."

"And I have to say that we are not really interested in buying a boat," said Lazarus.

The smile continued. Mr. Bayoumi did not look at all surprised.

"We have come on a more delicate matter," Lazarus continued. He eyed the toughs that stood nearby. "Perhaps you might like to discuss it more privately."

"Not at all," Bayoumi replied. "These are my most trusted employees."

"Very well. We are very interested in acquiring some ancient Egyptian artifacts. In particular, items fashioned in silver dating from the reign of Akhenaten. We were told that you were the man to speak with."

"Indeed? I must say that I am surprised by your request. The items you speak of are incredibly rare. So rare that only a handful know of their existence. I wonder, how is it that you two come to know of them?"

At this, Petrie couldn't resist getting involved in the exchange. "We are Egyptologists, sir. Items from the reign of the Heretic Pharaoh are noticeably scant. Naturally we seek such artifacts to fill in the gaps in our knowledge of the eighteenth dynasty."

"And yet you knew enough to know that they are made of silver. I wonder something else. If I were to call up the Antiquities Service, I would be able to speak with somebody who could verify your positions and your credentials? If I were to drop your names in conversation with Gaston Maspero he would be able to tell me something about you both?"

"Of course," replied Lazarus. "We are very well known in our fields."

Bayoumi's eyes flitted to Ahmed, who stood behind them. He said something in Arabic which Lazarus translated in his head too late. He knew the order to search them had been conveyed just as Ahmed's hands grasped his shoulders and one of the laborers came forward to check the pockets of his jacket.

"Sir! I must protest at this!" cried Petrie who was being held in a similar vice-like grip and was wriggling like a landed fish as his pockets were turned out.

Lazarus remained rigid, burning with rage, barely suppressed by the knowledge that it would be useless to put up a fight. They were dealing with gangsters—that was clear now—and to resist would only result in a beating, or worse.

Their captors finished turning them over and handed their wallets along with Lazarus's gun and Bowie knife to Bayoumi.

The Egyptian hefted the Colt thoughtfully. "A Colt Starblazer?" he said, impressed. "Very new and very expensive. An excellent weapon. Although an odd accessory for an Egyptologist."

"One never knows what rogues one might run into," said Lazarus through a thin smile.

Bayoumi rifled through their wallets, reading cards, examining documents and, of course, ignoring the money. Satisfied at last, he handed the wallets to one of his men to be returned to their rightful owners. He kept the gun and the knife.

"I can see at least that you do not belong to any agency of any great importance," said Bayoumi. "No spy would have such untidy wallets filled with so much useless paper. No, I think you are perhaps private detectives working in conjunction with the police, and that gives me a feeling of great relief. The Cairo police are such bunglers that they couldn't find a lost button, let alone a pair of inquisitive fools as you two. The Nile simply swallows up fools."

"Sir, I must warn you that this will be reported to the British Agent!" said Petrie.

Bayoumi smiled. "I think not." He looked to his men once more and spoke to them in Arabic. Lazarus was prepared this time and jumped out of his chair before Ahmed could put his hands on him once more. He drove the back of his skull into Ahmed's face. He felt something crunch satisfyingly and then was on his feet, swinging out with a right hook at the first man to come at him.

His fist connected with a jawbone, but he didn't have time to counter the savage blow with a blackjack that came whistling towards the left side of his head. Seeing stars, he reeled away, feeling his legs tripped by somebody and hearing the ringing laughter of Bayoumi as he went down.

The blow was not strong enough to knock him unconscious. He pressed the palms of his hands onto the dusty floor in an effort to gain his feet, but he was seized and hauled upright. He saw Petrie held in a similar position and was glad the Egyptologist had not put up a foolish fight as he had done.

They were dragged out through a different door than the one they had come in through. The warm air and the stink of the river greeted them. They found themselves on the top of a flight of steps that led down to the jetties on the other side of the building. Smaller boats were moored there, and their captors seemed intent on taking them down to one of them, no doubt planning to carry them out onto a quiet patch of water and do away with them.

As they made to descend the stone steps, Lazarus twisted in his captor's grip and let his balance go. They tumbled headfirst down the steps, the Egyptian's body beneath his own, to crash in a heap at the bottom.

Lazarus felt the grip on his arms slacken. He scrambled to his feet, not bothering to check if the man beneath him was unconscious or permanently silenced due to a broken neck. At the top of the steps, Petrie, inspired by Lazarus's courageous plunge, was attempting the same thing and succeeded in shaking himself loose from his captor's grip. He lifted up the toe of his shoe and jabbed it viciously into the groin of his foe. The man cried out and fell forward, one hand clutching for a grip and the other grasping the point of agony between his legs. Lazarus stood aside to let him roll past to join his companion at the foot of the steps.

"Come on, more will be coming!" Lazarus warned Petrie and together they took off, leaping over the twitching forms of their former captors.

They headed for the jetties. There was no other accessible place at the rear of the building without clambering over a high wall. Moving back through the warehouse was out of the question. Already three of Bayoumi's men were descending the steps, alarmed by the cries of their comrades.

"We might be able to lose them if we pinch one of their boats," said Lazarus as they pounded along the jetty, the boards groaning in protest at their passing.

They made for the one that was furthest out on the jetty and thus the farthest from land. It was a small, sad thing, little more than a rowing boat, although it did have a short mast and a sail furled up in the hull on top of what looked like a cargo of rugs.

They leapt into it and began fumbling at the

mooring rope. Lazarus wished he had his Bowie knife with him, and his revolver too for that matter, as the three Egyptians were nearly upon them. All he had to hand was an oar, and so he shoved off from the jetty, holding the oar out ready to clobber any of them that got too close.

They drifted out into Bulaq Harbor, waving at their pursuers. There was plenty of traffic on the Nile. *Dahabeahs* and smaller vessels weaved in and out, while heavy steamers drifted sluggishly past.

"How the hell do you steer this bloody thing?" yelled Petrie, tugging at ropes as they headed straight into the line of traffic.

"Christ, watch out!" Lazarus shouted, leaping down into the bilge and seizing the rudder. They narrowly missed the tail end of a *dahabeah*, ignoring the curses of its captain and the amused stares of its European passengers, and ploughed deeper into the confusing array of vessels.

"Raise the sail!" said Lazarus. "We're hopelessly adrift without it!"

Not much of a sailor, Petrie eventually managed to hoist the triangular sail according to Lazarus's shouted and increasingly impatient instructions. As the wind filled it, Lazarus tacked and cut a path through the traffic.

They emerged in the wider lane occupied by steamers of various sizes, loaded with tourists and cargoes headed to Alexandria and Stamboul. "For God's sake don't hit anything!" Petrie wailed.

"I'll do my best," Lazarus replied through gritted teeth.

They passed within five yards of a steamer and found themselves bobbing up and down like a cork in its wake. The bow of the vessel dipped alarmingly, and they took on water as a wave crashed over the gunwale.

"Get bailing!" Lazarus shouted. "Find a bucket!"

Petrie began to search between the rolled-up rugs for a bucket as the boom swept over his head. They had lost the wind in the hard tack to avoid the collision and Lazarus was desperately trying to find it again. A horn blared out a warning as another steamer came towards them. Lazarus panicked and tacked again, but the steamer's captain was already changing his course to avoid hitting them. The huge white side of the steamer with its wheel-like paddles thundering water drifted towards them like the white cliffs of Dover. Lazarus let the rudder slip from his fingers. There was no avoiding this one. They would collide; their puny vessel against several hundred tons of paddle steamer.

Petrie poked his head up out of the hold, waving a bucket about, his face triumphant. "Look!" he cried. "I've found one!"

Chapter Four

In which an old acquaintance appears in the nick of time

"The theft of a boat," said the police captain as he went over the report in his hand. "Violence, vandalism and disruption of traffic in the harbor. Not to mention nearly sinking a steamer carrying over two hundred passengers, and I haven't got to the real juicy part yet."

"Oh?" said Lazarus.

They were in a small, untidy office. The nametag on the desk read 'Captain Hassanein'. The man behind that nametag was a portly fellow with a brick-shaped face sporting a few day's grey stubble. Their handcuffs had been removed only because there were two policemen standing guard in the corridor outside.

Miraculously, their stolen vessel had not been smashed into thousands of pieces upon contact with the steamer. It had been wrecked for sure and set to bob about like driftwood, its mast snapped and its sail covering its dazed crew. By the time they had managed to pull the canvas off their faces, they found themselves looking up into the eyes of a dozen policemen who had been dispatched in a similar vessel to apprehend the two hooligans who were causing so much trouble.

"We have been trying to break the ring of black

market antiquities dealers for some years now," went on Captain Hassanein. "I can honestly say that I am surprised that two Englishmen were so deeply involved. Of course, it is to be expected that the English had some hand in it—natural thieves as you are, plundering the treasures of other countries like common pirates. And you sir, an Egyptologist," he looked at Petrie. "A thief masquerading as a man of learning in order to steal from our country. Disgraceful."

"Now wait just a minute," Petrie protested. "What's all this about stolen antiquities?"

The police captain ignored him and continued. "Clearly you were hoping to ship the items north and then transfer them to a vessel heading to Europe. Frankly, I don't care about the details. What I want to know is where you got the items. One could suggest that you discovered the tomb from which they came and told no one, but I think it unlikely. If your skills as archaeologists are anything like your skills as sailors, then I doubt either one of you could find a beetle under a rock. I must assume that you know persons who themselves have kept this hidden tomb a secret for many years and sell off bits at a time to avoid detection." He smiled. "That plan would seem to have failed in their association with you two."

"We don't know what you're talking about," said Lazarus. "It is true that we entered the premises of Bayoumi Shipping looking for antiquities, but we wished only to identify the culprits in this black market in order to help you with your case."

At this, the police chief smiled, clearly not believing a word of it. "How very generous of you."

"Bayoumi is certainly the man you're after," Lazarus

continued. "He all but admitted that he had items to sell. He uses his contacts to ship them out of the country. After interviewing us he tried to have us killed. We escaped and fled taking one of his boats with us."

"Yes, a boat waiting for you all loaded up with its cargo," came the reply. "Very convenient."

"If you like an abundance of carpets," said Lazarus.

"An abundance of carpets containing thousands of pounds worth of antiquities."

"What?" both Lazarus and Petrie exclaimed in unison, gaping at him.

"We have unfurled every carpet found on board. Cheap, local junk mostly, but the perfect disguise for your true cargo. In the centre of each roll was a trinket—necklaces, ushabtis, armbands, statuettes— enough to please Mr. Maspero and assure him that we are winning the war over those who wish to rob this country blind of its heritage."

Lazarus and Petrie were speechless. The evidence against them was staggering and they could see no way out. Lazarus spoke at last. "Look, sir, I know my right to make requests is somewhat limited at present but I ask you only one thing. Put in a call to the British Agent. Tell Baring that you have one of Morton's men in your custody. That's all I ask, a simple telephone call."

"Your British Agent can't help you now," said the police chief. "He's far too busy meddling in our customs and extorting our Khedive to care for a couple of fellow thieves from his homeland. Now, I am a realistic man, I know that as British citizens I will eventually be forced to turn you over to the military or perhaps the secret police, but in the meantime I intend to learn all I can from you using all the methods at my fingertips." He let the silence hang as a threat.

Lazarus knew all too well the brutalities inflicted on suspects in the bowels of the Cairo police station in order to get a confession and decided that it was best to remain silent for the time being.

They were taken away and returned to their cell, which was of the communal variety and contained twelve other prisoners, mostly Egyptians. There was a single bucket for urine and feces which succeeded in filling the small cell with an unholy stink. It was crowded, hot, dark and ugly and served to increase the desperation of anybody on the wrong side of its heavy, bolted door.

"This is monstrous!" exclaimed Petrie as somebody jolted the bucket of feces for the second time in under five minutes. "What on earth will become of us? Our careers, our reputations, not to mention our very lives! Will they execute us, do you think?"

"Calm yourself, Petrie," said Lazarus. "They can't do anything to us but keep us here for the night. As British subjects we do not fall under their jurisdiction. They must hand us over to the consulate in the morning, where I can make the arrangements for all this to be cleared up. But for the time being we must be patient."

This seemed to fortify the Egyptologist somewhat, but he did not stop his weak protestations. "I'll never live this down!" he kept saying under his breath. "Me! One of England's leading Egyptologists spending a night in the clink!"

Several hours passed and Lazarus and Petrie began to wonder if it was possible to get any sleep standing upright. Suddenly a key grated in the lock and the door to the cell swung open eliciting cries of hope from everybody within. The sound was pitiful, like hearing cries of the damned from some dark pit in Hell. The muzzle of a rifle poked into the cell and orders barked in Arabic warned the prisoners to hold back. Lazarus and Petrie's names were called out and they stepped forward cautiously, hoping against all the odds that they were being released, or at least transferred early. But at the back of their minds lurked the dread of interrogation.

They were led up to the chief's office where they found Hassanein wearing an even deeper frown than the one he had had on earlier. He extended a hand to the two chairs in front of his desk and they sat down, gasping with relief at the easing of their leg muscles.

"It appears that you have friends in high places," said Hassanein. "Or at least you are something more than the common thieves I took you for, even if you are as stupid."

Lazarus remained silent, not wishing to ruin whatever godsend this was with an impertinent remark.

"Whatever your interest in Bayoumi Shipping was, it no longer concerns me," the captain went on. "What I am interested in is all you know of the black market in antiquities. What led you to Mr. Bayoumi?"

Lazarus cleared his throat. He was not about to let slip more than he had to to this incompetent and most likely corrupt tool of the Khedivate. "Are we to be released?"

"Under my severest protestations," Captain Hassanein answered.

"Then we are under no obligation to tell you anything. I presume you did as I requested and contacted Major Baring?"

"No, I did not."

"Then how…?"

"Because somebody had to step in and save your hide once again," came a woman's voice from behind them.

Lazarus and Petrie jumped in their seats and swiveled around to see a woman lounging like a panther in an armchair that had been screened by the door when they had come in. Her hair was black and bound up high. She was smoking a cigarette held in a long holder, gripped lightly between ivory fingers.

"Katarina!" gasped Lazarus.

"Longman," she purred with a smile.

"Miss Mikolavna from the Russian intelligence services has been helping us with our case against the black marketeers," said Hassanein.

"Sounds a tad trivial for the Okhrana," said Lazarus, knowing that his use of the word would irritate Katarina who denied the existence of such an agency.

"Come now, Longman," she said, "Am I supposed to believe that your superiors sent you here to catch sellers of mummified hands and stone beetles? I have my mission and you have yours. This black market business clearly signals some overlap in our pursuits. Once again."

"And as the representative of the police here in Cairo," said the captain, "I am naturally the last to know anything."

Lazarus could not suppress a smile. Somebody had certainly let the hot air out of the poor police captain. In just a few hours he had gone from being the man holding all the cards to a mere eavesdropper on the activities of people in far higher positions than him.

Lazarus rose and Petrie joined him. "Well, if there's nothing else, I would like to go back to my hotel and freshen up. I've had a most educational tour of the Cairo Police headquarters, but I don't wish to take up any more of your time, Captain. Good day!"

"Hold it right there," said the captain in a voice that sounded like he was desperately trying to claw back some authority as his only lead in his case was about to walk out through his door. "We need some information from you. How did you know about Bayoumi Shipping? Who sent you there?"

"Sorry, Captain," said Lazarus with a smile. "I don't reveal my sources in case I wish to use them again. And as you have no charges against either my associate or I, we are under no obligation to aid you in your investigation. Katarina, thank you for your intervention. We are much obliged."

The captain rose and slammed his hand down on his desk as they walked out of the door. "You might be a free man today, Ingleezeh! But if I find out that you are in any way connected to the selling of antiquities, I will have you back in my cells so quick your head will be spinning! And you won't have this Russian woman to help you a second time!"

Lazarus and Petrie ignored him as they left his office and headed downstairs to the street where the bustle of morning was beginning to thrum. Lazarus's head was feverish, but it had nothing to do with the steadily increasing heat or his night in the pestilent cells. *Katarina Mikolavna*! He had not dared himself to imagine that he would ever see her again, to hear her soft eastern tones or inhale her beautiful scent. She was just as acidic, just as spiteful and just as wonderful as she had been a year ago. To think what the fates were planning by having their paths cross once more!

Petrie also seemed bowled over by the Russian

agent's sudden appearance. "Who the devil was that, Lazarus?" he demanded as they crossed the street. "You obviously know each other."

"That, my dear friend, was Katarina Mikolavna. The Russian I met in America last year."

Petrie's eyes goggled at him. "The enemy agent who helped you out? You never said it was a woman!"

True enough, Lazarus had kept the gender of his Russian comrade vague when he had related his adventures to Petrie. For some reason he felt that it was almost as secret as the fact that they really did find the seven golden cities of Cibola. Also, it made the tale of his trip to New York and Boston in the stolen airship—the *Santa Bella*—easier to explain.

Petrie seemed to remember that particular part of his tale at just that moment and his eyes widened even more. "You and she shared a balloon together? One of those little ones with bunks?"

Lazarus smiled and nodded.

"My God, man! That woman! That hair! Those lips! And, oh! That accent! You must have a constitution of steel to see such a voyage through without losing your mind and throwing yourself upon her!"

"Who is to say I didn't?" said Lazarus with a smile.

That shut Petrie up and they continued in silence, the glow on the Egyptologist's cheeks speaking enough for both of them.

They headed back to their respective hotels and, once in his room, Lazarus stripped off, shaved and drew himself a hot bath. He retrieved the bottle of gin from his portmanteau and poured himself a generous measure before slipping into the almost painfully hot water with a great sigh. As the heat penetrated his bones, he sipped his drink and enjoyed the stinging taste of London's streets; a pleasant memory here amidst the dirt, dust and heat of the Egyptian capital.

That afternoon Lazarus found a message had been left for him at reception.

```
LONGMAN
MEET ME AT THE CAFE ON EL
MAGHRABI TWO O CLOCK. WE NEED TO
DISCUSS THINGS
KATARINA
```

Lazarus knew the café. He didn't go inside, but instead hung around beneath the arches where a water seller was doing good business. After a while he spotted Katarina, her pale face shielded by a black parasol and her skirts hemmed just right so that they wouldn't trail in the dust. She had seen him and came over to the shade of the arches.

"Won't you come inside for a coffee?" she asked him.

"Coffee? Yes, well it would be lovely to catch up, but I didn't suppose that was why you wanted to see me. Besides, it wouldn't be proper for an unmarried couple to sit in a café together."

She stared at him. "Amazing. Two weeks together in a balloon, a shared secret about cities of gold that we can never tell anybody, and you still have your damned English attitude towards conventions. Very well, I'll say what I have to say to you here under these arches. I have just come from the police station. Our friend, Captain Hassanein sent his men round to Bayoumi

Shipping this morning after you left and found the place deserted. Bayoumi must have panicked at your arrest and has shut up shop."

"Doesn't surprise me really," said Lazarus. "Will you go looking for him?"

She shook her head. "No point. There are a hundred such businessmen who export antiquities out of this country. Squashing one won't make a jot of difference. We need to go after the men who sell the items to the dealers; the ones who steal them from their original locations."

Lazarus sighed. "Isn't it about time you dropped the act now?"

She frowned. "How do you mean?"

"I mean, I would have to be a man with a turnip for a brain if I were to believe that you had been sent here from Moscow to chase around black market dealers."

"And what do you know of my orders?"

"I can make a fair stab in the dark. Your orders are to find Dr. Rutherford Lindholm and drag him back to your country so your government can pry open his brain and learn his secrets. You found out, as I did, that the only trail to him was through the black market, only you don't have any contacts in that world and so the trail for you ran cold. Now you need my help in finding it again."

"Well, what of it?" she said coldly. "It wouldn't be the first time that we have worked together."

"No. And it wouldn't be the first time that we have sought the same man for our respective governments. Why do we always end up on opposite sides of the fence?"

"That's the way of the world, Longman. Maybe if your government would give up its support for the blasted C.S.A. we might become friends."

"Britain will never support the Union," said Lazarus. "It's not financially sound."

"As always, the great decisions of the world come down to money. Enough of politics. Will you help me?"

"If I do then it must be on my terms."

"As you say."

"I know a man. My loyalty to him has run out as I have a feeling that it was he who led my friend and I into a trap at Bayoumi's. Nevertheless, I don't want him in the hands of the police. I can do without the reputation as a snitch for the likes of Captain Hassanein."

"How can this man help us?"

"I can interrogate him. Or follow him. I've an idea that with Bayoumi gone he will go running to his sources to tell them that he needs time to find another customer. They'll be fellahs most likely, perhaps working on a dig somewhere, hopefully for Lindholm. We just need to keep our distance and see where he leads us. Where are you staying?"

"The Grand."

"Good. So is Petrie. I will find out what I can and get word to you when the time is right."

"All right. I must be getting along. It's a shame we didn't have that coffee. It's been a long time."

"Yes," agreed Lazarus as she walked away. She turned and looked at him from beneath the frills of her parasol. He thought she was going to say that it was good to see him again for something similar was on the tip of his own tongue.

"Longman?"

"Yes?"

"No tricks this time."

Chapter Five

In which a significantly longer voyage is undertaken

The house where Murad was staying was reflective of the whole area. It was a crumbling tenement with pokey, dark windows from which washing dangled. The sturdy-looking door was the only thing that looked solid about the whole structure.

Lazarus had been given the address by the proprietor of the café they had met Murad in two nights ago. He had slipped the man a couple of piastres to keep his mouth shut and not let on to Murad that he was looking for him.

Dawn was breaking over the rooftops of Cairo, and Lazarus rubbed his eyes. He had been standing on the street corner for over an hour, dressed in the shabby clothes of a European on his uppers to deter the Cairenes from asking him for *baksheesh*. He kept a good supply of outfits for various occasions in his hotel room and found they invariably came in useful for situations such as these.

At last, the door to the house opened and Murad slipped out, like a rat emerging from its hole. Murad was not a Cairene and relied upon the generosity of friends and the vulnerability of women to sleep soundly whenever he was in the city. This made him a hard man to track, but Lazarus knew the right people and his hour of standing in the cold had paid off.

Resisting the urge to creep up on the villain and throttle him from behind, Lazarus followed Murad down endless streets and passageways where vendors were beginning to set up shop for the day. Cafes were starting to open, the scent of their freshly brewed coffee allowed to drift out and draw in the first customers of the day.

They drew near to the docks and Lazarus's hopes rose. He had imagined the dealer would need passage on a vessel heading south to wherever his contacts dwelled, and he had hoped that Murad would make his move this morning. The chaos of Port Bulaq was no less at any time of day. Soon Lazarus found he had a job keeping up with his quarry as he was jostled from side to side by lost travelers, fellahs importing goods, urchins and pickpockets. He managed to keep one eye on the back of Murad's tarboosh as it ducked down a side street.

He followed him, pushing his way past a man struggling with a cart load of tomatoes, diving into the ally where beggars held out their hands in a permanent state of helplessness. To his dismay, he could no longer see Murad. He broke into a jog.

The alley emerged onto a wharf where several transport agencies had set up business. Any one of them might offer the young Egyptian passage on a steamer or a *dahabeah*, but Lazarus guessed that Murad would choose one of the more run-down looking ones, partly because he was not a wealthy foreigner and partly because he would wish to remain inconspicuous.

He headed for the most slapdash looking outfit, which had its name painted freehand in both Arabic and miss-spelt English on the side of its rough wall. He went indoors. The man at the desk looked up from his ledger as if he had just finished penning something in.

"Do you have any vessels heading up the Nile today or tomorrow?" Lazarus asked the man.

"Assuredly, *effendi*," said the clerk, eyeing Lazarus's clothes as if he was evaluating whether the term of respect was warranted in this case. "How far do you wish to go?"

"Oh, we haven't made up our minds yet, I, my wife and my friend, that is. Luxor at least. Perhaps as far as Abu Simbel. My wife wants to see those headless pharaohs or whatever they are."

The clerk nearly rolled his eyes but saved himself just in time. He was clearly disgusted by this shabby European who didn't even have enough coin to his name to be a Cook's tourist, but not so disgusted that he would turn away his custom. "The *Nefertiti* leaves tomorrow morning at eight of the clock. Is that too early for you?"

"Not at all," said Lazarus. "Put me down for three tickets."

"Very well, I will just go and write them out then I will take down your details. A moment's patience if you please."

When the clerk disappeared into the back room, Lazarus leaned over and pulled the ledger towards him. It was open on the page of the *Nefertiti*'s passenger list. He ran his index finger down the page, scanning the names until he arrived at 'Murad Yasin' and knew that he had at least found the right company and the right vessel.

He whiled away the afternoon taking tea in Azbekya Gardens and packing his portmanteau. Evening had set in by the time he arrived at the Grand Continental Hotel. He left a message at reception for Katarina to meet him first thing in the morning at Port Bulaq. He considered trying to obtain her room number and asking her down for drinks or perhaps dinner but knew he would feel like a cad if he did. She was exactly right about him, he realized. They had slept under the Arizona stars together and traversed a continent in a balloon, eating their meals at a small table and bunking in the same tiny cabin by the light of a single gas lamp, but here, in a passable example of civilization, he dared not ask her to dinner without a chaperone for fear of violating propriety.

He instead went to Petrie's room and the two of them sipped cognacs while Lazarus explained the events of the day to him.

"Up for another adventure?" he asked the Egyptologist when he was finished.

Petrie's eyes twinkled but his brow was furrowed at the same time, as if he was fighting with himself. "Will it be dangerous?"

"Undoubtedly."

"And that Russian woman will be coming?"

Lazarus's eyes briefly rolled. "Yes. She's a damned fine shot if that will make you feel any safer."

"Oh, undoubtedly, undoubtedly," Petrie said, stroking his beard thoughtfully. "But perhaps it would be safer for her if two men were to accompany her. I have a mind to purchase a revolver after yesterday's encounter with those villains. I shall make enquiries first thing tomorrow."

"Then you will come? Your knowledge of Akhenaten's reign and religious movement may be invaluable to us if we do indeed find Rousseau's site."

This comment seemed to galvanize the young scholar. "Absolutely! I could not pass up an opportunity such as this! Imagine what secrets of the eighteenth dynasty a new site might unlock! The Silver Aten... The mind positively boggles!" He knocked down the rest of his cognac and spilled some as if he had suddenly remembered something. "That reminds me! I've been looking at my sketches—I always do them, you know, of my finds—including the ones that were stolen. And something has occurred to me."

"Show me," Lazarus said.

Petrie went over to his writing desk which was littered with bits of paper, books and sketchpads, and drew out a couple of sheaves with some drawings on them. They were very good ones, done with the painstaking attention to detail that Petrie was known for. Lazarus studied them.

"That's a kohl container I found at Tell el-Amarna," said Petrie, indicating the first sketch. "The one stolen from my poor man at the docks. Imagine that it was dropped nearly three thousand years ago by a lady at Akhenaten's court, to lie in the sand after the city's destruction, unseen by generations upon generations until I picked it up! Only to be stolen by an unknown murderer!"

Lazarus examined the drawing of the tube-shaped artifact once used to contain the black substance the Ancient Egyptians painted their eyelids with. Some hieroglyphics were engraved vertically along the length of the tube but before Lazarus could decipher them Petrie slid another sketch in front of him.

"This is the sketch I did of the fragment I found and gave to Maspero's museum. Also now stolen, of course."

It was a relief fragment showing part of a woman's head wearing a Nubian wig surrounded by hieroglyphics. Lazarus tried to read them and found that one of the hieroglyphics had been entirely obliterated, as if deliberately.

"It was not uncommon for the names of the deceased to be scratched off monuments by people who were angry with them," said Lazarus. "Akhenaten for instance, had the majority of his monuments defaced by his descendants. In fact, it's a wonder we know his name at all. Without a name the deceased cannot find peace in the afterlife and is doomed to wander in limbo for all eternity, or so they once believed."

"Quite so," agreed Petrie, producing yet another sketch for him. "Fortunately, the hieroglyph on this relief fragment was not wholly destroyed. One cannot make it out in the sketch, so I did a separate reproduction of just the damaged hieroglyph. Look here."

Lazarus looked. "Seems to be part of a feather and the tip of a bird's head. There doesn't look to have been a cartouche surrounding them, so the person probably wasn't royalty."

"No. But compare the damaged hieroglyph to the one on the kohl container."

Lazarus took his time, not jumping to the conclusion that Petrie had so obviously drawn. But he had to admit, the symbols could have been the same. The kohl container had two feathers, a bowl, a bird and a couple of slanted strokes. He mouthed the phonetic values of the symbols; "Kiya."

"Kiya." Petrie confirmed.

"The name doesn't ring any bells, I'm afraid. You?"

"Not a jingle, but she must have made somebody very angry to have had her name scratched off this relief like that. It's quite possible that the lady in the Nubian wig on the relief is this Kiya—the very Kiya who once owned the kohl container."

"I'm not sure where all this is leading us," Lazarus confessed.

Petrie sighed. "Nor I. But Kiya—whoever she was—must have been somebody of great importance at Akhetaten to appear on a relief like this, so beautifully painted… but then to have her name stolen from her, so to speak."

"Who do you think she was?"

"Who knows? Perhaps one of Akhenaten's wives or daughters. He had several of each, you know. We only know a handful of their names. Meriaten and Meketaten were two of his daughters, reflecting his habit for including the sun god's name in the names of all members of his family. Apart from his great royal wife Queen Nefertiti, we don't know of any other wives or consorts, but he probably had several. They often did."

"Yes, as well as that repugnant habit of marrying their siblings," said Lazarus.

"Indeed. Whoever this Kiya was, she may have been tied up in the family of the Heretic Pharaoh in more ways than one. And perhaps our journey on the morrow will reveal her true identity as well as shed more light on Akhenaten's reign. I only showed you these sketches because I find it so odd that both items stolen seemed to bear the name of Kiya. Coincidence, perhaps, but still…"

"Yes," agreed Lazarus. "Still…"

Katarina had got Lazarus's message, and was waiting for him with her usual punctuality on the dock of the appropriately named *Nefertiti*. Her beauty was a stark contrast to the state of the steamer that was to take them up the Nile and Lazarus's jaw dropped when he saw it. It was a wreck.

He was put in mind of the *Mary Sue*—that floating nest of villains he had penetrated on the Colorado River. This one was smaller but just as filthy, with rust streaking its once-white sides and its blackened, cancerous funnels caked with soot.

"It was on such a vessel that we first met, Katarina," said Lazarus, trying to be jovial. "Do you remember?"

"I remember trying to kill you," the Russian replied.

"Yes, well, we know each other a bit better now, eh?"

"That doesn't mean that I will let you take Dr. Lindholm from me without a fight. Pray it doesn't come to that."

Flinders Petrie was hailing them as he made his way down the dock, a servant lugging his case a few paces behind.

"Good morning, Lazarus!" he cried with all the excitement of a schoolboy on holiday. "And Miss Mikolavna! Lazarus has told me all about you!"

"Has he?" Katarina said, eyeing Lazarus coolly.

Lazarus gave her a look to reassure her that he had most certainly not told Petrie *everything* about her.

"You have my eternal thanks, madam," said Petrie, doffing his straw hat and bowing low, "for getting Lazarus and I out of that loathsome prison. I cannot thank you enough."

"Don't mention it," replied Katarina, allowing, with much reluctance, the Egyptologist to kiss her hand.

"And may I say that it is the highest of pleasures to be travelling with such a jewel of a woman. Queen Cleopatra herself would pale in comparison to your exotic complexion!"

"I think we had best be getting on board and finding our cabins," said Katarina. "Egyptians are not punctual by anyone's standards, but the vessel will no doubt be leaving sometime soon, and the sooner the better as far as I am concerned."

Petrie insisted on carrying Katarina's small carpetbag up the gangplank and tottered after her, trying to carry on his flattery. "I may not have military experience like Lazarus here, Miss Mikolavna," he said, but I know how to shoot a gun and have one close to my person at all times! There is no need to fear anything while I am near you!" He made to draw an antique-looking pistol out of his breeches to show her, but Lazarus darted forward to stay his hand.

"Don't go waving artillery about, for God's sake, man! We are not here to attract attention."

"Quite right, Lazarus, quite right. Apologies. I was merely carried away by the scent of adventure in my nostrils, and the thought of any harm stepping into the vicinity of our dear Miss Mikolavna brings out the primal beast in me."

Lazarus inspected the revolver. It was a Colt Army Model 1860. "Where did you get that relic, anyway? It's at least twenty years old!"

"A fellow at the hotel put me in the direction of a salesman. Nothing wrong with a tried and tested weapon."

Lazarus himself had purchased an Enfield Mark II;

the favored revolver of the British army and his previous weapon of choice before he had acquired the Colt Starblazer. The loss of that magnificent weapon still stung him. He would have to place an order with Morton for a new one as soon as he got back to London, if not before. He briefly wondered if Katarina still kept that long-barreled Smith and Wesson Model Russian strapped to her thigh and smiled at the thought of it.

They went to find their cabins which contained a couple of grubby mattresses on bunks connected by a wooden ladder that looked to give anybody climbing it in bare feet a nasty splinter. On the wall, a cockroach made a quick scurry for cover as Lazarus dumped his portmanteau on the bare floor.

"You're down the hall, Flinders," he said. "You can leave Katarina's case here."

"I beg your pardon?" Katarina asked. Her eyes were dangerously wide and Lazarus knew that expression never bode well. "Am I to assume that you've taken it upon yourself to bunk with me?"

"Well, I thought it would seem more proper if we were to travel as man and wife…" he began feebly.

"Man and wife. Let me guess. Proprieties? Convention? I am beginning to wonder if all Englishmen simply use these things to their own advantage. You can take your case out of here, Longman, and bloody well find somewhere else to sleep!"

"But I only booked three bunks!" Lazarus protested, suddenly finding himself standing in the corridor holding his portmanteau. "Everywhere else is taken, I'm sure!"

"Improvise!" came the Russian's retort as the door

slammed in his face.

"Katarina, this is ridiculous!" he shouted through the woodwork. "God knows we've roughed it together over more nights than I can count, now is no time to be prudish!"

He was aware of a couple of men in tourist attire sniggering as they walked past. Petrie was watching him sorrowfully from down the hall. "You would be more than welcome to bunk with me, Lazarus, only I seem to be sharing with somebody already," he called, indicating the large Egyptian man who had elbowed his way past into the cabin and was currently heaving himself up onto the top bunk.

"Never mind," Lazarus said. "I'll find a spot on deck. If it's good enough for the crew, it's good enough for me. It'll be a fine night, I'm sure."

CHAPTER SIX

**In which our heroes find themselves up the Nile
without a paddle steamer**

I t was not a fine night, much to Lazarus's dismay. His ideas of watching the stars pass overhead as the warm wind drifted from the palms on the bank were dashed by a thick cloud cover that masked even the moon, and a chill wind that kept him shivering as he lay on the hard deck with nothing but his overcoat as a blanket.

The day had been a long and frustrating one. The steamer was no Thomas Cook cruise, and the compromise in price was showed in its itinerary, which eliminated all but the most crucially important sites along the Nile. Their first stop was the pyramids of Gizah, merely hours after their departure. Posing as tourists, Lazarus and his companions could hardly refuse the donkey ride to the pyramids, Mariette's house and the Serapeum, even though both Lazarus and Petrie could have told the barely comprehensible guides more than a thing or two about the sites. Katarina was the only one of the trio who had never seen them before, and she seemed genuinely interested in the histories of the Great Pyramid of Khufu and the mysterious Sphinx which was, at present, surrounded by the dig site of Maspero.

Petrie enjoyed himself a little too much and had to

be stifled on more than one occasion when he began to relate his methods of measuring the pyramids, nearly giving them away in the process. Even Lazarus had to admit that it was a refreshing rush to be back at the site that had fascinated him as a child, ever since he had seen an etching of the pyramids in a book in his guardian's library. Here, in the sands of the desert, surrounded by the crumbling ruins of a civilization nearly forgotten, the world seemed simpler. They were a million miles from the scheming of governments and clandestine missions handed out by shadowy authorities in European capitals.

Disaster had nearly struck when they returned to the steamer. Several of the travelers had remained aboard, not wishing to join the excursion. One of these was Murad, who emerged from his cabin just as Lazarus, Katarina and Petrie rounded the corner. Lazarus immediately steered them away as Murad sauntered past, not even blinking. Bumping into their quarry had always been a danger, and Lazarus swore that he would make sure all three of them were more careful in future.

The cold wind of the night, coupled with the chugging of the steamer's paddles, meant that sleep felt like a hopelessly ambitious goal. Lazarus eventually gave up and went in search of warmth and something to drink.

He found both beneath the overhang of the cabins where several Americans, British and one Frenchman were sitting out playing cards and drinking whiskey. Being no greenhorn when it came to the game of Faro, Lazarus struck up conversation and soon earned himself a seat at the table and a hand in the next round. Cheerful small talk was not really his forte, but the sight of the whiskey bottle on the table urged him to great exertions in the art of polite conversation. Soon he was rewarded with a glass of the amber nectar that warmed his aching bones and made the thought of sleeping on deck not quite so dreadful.

The following day proved more eventful, despite most of it being used up by chugging upriver with nothing to see until they were due at Minieh later that evening. The banks slid past; palm trees, swathes of Halfeh grass and tamarisks, punctuated by the occasional small village from which the inhabitants would usually swarm into the water up to their waists, some even swimming out to the passing ships to ask for *baksheesh*. But the sight of the clapped-out *Nefertiti* and its assorted passengers hailing from the lower orders of various nations evidently persuaded most villagers that it was not worth getting their feet wet.

Lazarus and Petrie leaned on the rail, smoking and watching the land drift past, sharing stories and laughing at their old days of poking around in temples and tombs. Katarina was in her cabin reading. It was Petrie who first spotted the danger and discreetly brought Lazarus's attention to it.

"Psst! Did you see him?"

Lazarus knew enough to keep his head firmly pointed forwards and not to swivel around to gape at whatever his companion was getting at. "No. What is it?"

"Look carefully, to the left, at who just walked past us."

Lazarus slowly tuned his head as if interested in a heron that had just caught a fish on the bank. Further down the deck, dressed in a tarboosh and simple business clothes, was a man instantly recognizable to both Lazarus and Petrie, for barely a few days had passed since they had been detained at his leisure in the Cairo police station.

"Christ! What's he doing here?" Lazarus hissed. But it was a foolish question and he knew it. There was only one reason for Captain Hassanein to be aboard the same steamer other than an outrageously wild coincidence, and that was that he was after their quarry.

"Who's he talking to?" Petrie said.

The unidentified man stood with his back to them, but his dress and the pale skin of his bald head suggested that he was not an Egyptian. When he turned, they saw the large waxed moustache that dominated his face, and Petrie let out a gasp of recognition.

"Émile Brugsch!"

"Isn't he the brother of Heinrich Brugsch?" asked Lazarus, "who used to be the head of the School of Egyptology in Cairo?"

"Yes, until that institution closed down and Heinrich moved back to Prussia," said Petrie. "Émile is his brother's junior by fifteen years and was Mariette's keenest protégé. He was rumbled selling artifacts from the museum's basement and should have been sent packing there and then, if you ask me. But Mariette gave him another chance and gave him the position of museum conservator, and he has been working with the police in cracking the black market in antiquities."

"It takes one to know one, it seems. Well, there's no ambiguity as to why these two are onboard," said Lazarus.

"Yes, but how the devil did they get onto Murad's trail? He's *our* lead, or so I thought."

"I know damn well how they came to be here," said Lazarus bitterly. He swung away from the rail and, careful to keep his face hidden from Hassanein and Brugsch, made his way towards Katarina's cabin.

He hammered on the door with enough force to crack the old wood. When it failed to open immediately, he bellowed through the woodwork as if hoping that would shatter it. "Get out here, Mikolavna! You've got to explain yourself! I won't be fobbed off any longer!"

"I say, keep it down, old chap!" said an Englishman, poking his head out of a door further down the corridor. "Your rows with your missus are your own affair but kindly leave the rest of us out of it!"

Lazarus ignored him and hammered again. Eventually the door opened, and Katarina looked out at him. "Gracious, you do have a pulse after all," she said, with the glimmer of a rare smile on her lips.

"Just what the devil do you mean by it, woman?" Lazarus demanded.

"By what, you oaf? Hammering on a lady's door like it was a public house!"

"By letting that blasted police captain in on things?"

Katarina's eyes narrowed. "I don't know what you're talking about."

"I just saw him, damn it! And that Brugsch fellow too! You told them all about our tailing of Murad after I specifically said I didn't want to involve the police."

"Speak sense, Longman. What possible reason would I have for wanting the police involved? You yourself acknowledged that my mission had nothing to do with the black market. If anything, I would want those fools well away from this as their presence will only compromise us."

Lazarus took in her words but did not relinquish her from his angry glare. "Well how the hell did they know to follow Murad?" he said at last.

"I imagine they had either you or your companion followed," she replied. "You're not as inconspicuous as you seem to think. Following you would have been my first port of call also."

"Well, we're buggered now, pardon the language. If Murad spots those idiots, he'll be off like a jackrabbit and we'll be left scratching our arses."

"Then I suggest you do everything in your power to prevent him from seeing either Hassanein or yourselves."

"While you'll be in your cabin reading, I suppose?"

"Best to keep a low profile."

"Perhaps we could keep a low profile together," Lazarus suggested and then realized how it sounded, and colored. "Well, you've got an empty bunk in there and one of those buggers is liable to bloody well trip over me on deck if he decides to take a midnight stroll."

Katarina rolled her eyes. "You wouldn't be trying to weasel your way into my bedchamber on exaggerated grounds would you, Longman?"

"I paid for the bloody cabin!"

"Very well," she said, flinging the door open wide. She was wearing a thin silk garment which made Lazarus's eyes goggle. "Make yourself at home. Top bunk's yours."

They drifted into Minieh in the early evening. Most of the passengers disembarked to explore the city. In the morning, many of them would go on to the tombs at Beni Hassan while the steamer took on fresh food.

Lazarus dispatched Katarina to watch Murad's

cabin and to alert him if there was any movement. There wasn't, and they bedded down at around eleven o'clock.

When the passengers returned the following day, they set off once more and a further day of solid travelling was undertaken. There was still no sign of Murad, and Lazarus began to worry that he had given them the slip at Minieh.

But when the boat drew up at the quays of Bellianah, Katarina reported that Murad had emerged from his cabin with his suitcase in tow. Lazarus sighed with relief. "At last we can ditch this godforsaken steamer and hopefully Hassanein and Brugsch in the bargain!"

Bellianah was the port of call for those wishing to see the ruined temples at Abydus. They joined the mob who were about to depart and were provided with donkeys for the excursion. They saw that Murad was attempting the same trick, and nobody seemed to notice that he had loaded his bag behind the saddle.

"Maybe he wants to see the funeral chapel of Seti I," joked Petrie, who had long expressed a desire to excavate at Abydus, convinced there was more to find there.

But any hopes to see the pillared temples once more were dashed by Murad's quick departure from the group as soon as they set foot out of the village. His tarboosh wavering back and forth atop his donkey, Murad wobbled towards a cluster of palm trees, letting the tourists drift on without him. Lazarus and his companions halted also and led their donkeys around the side of a granary, keeping out of sight. Lazarus grew aware of another pair of travelers watching them from the outskirts of the village, and he cursed as he recognized the police captain and the museum conservator.

"Is there no giving them the slip?" he grumbled.

"Look!" said Petrie, "He's on the move!"

Murad was heading off through the palms in a southerly direction, following the riverbank.

"Best to hold back for a time," said Katarina, opening her black parasol to fend off the afternoon rays. "We don't want him seeing the three of us trotting after him."

"You should perhaps give our friends a lesson in stealth," said Petrie, indicating Captain Hassanein and his companion who were off following Murad's trail so close they might as well be travelling with him. Lazarus cursed again.

"Although," mused Petrie, "Murad won't necessarily recognize them. Maybe it's best to have them as a buffer. That way we can follow them rather than him. It's more discreet."

"There's nothing discreet about six city folk on donkeys heading in the same direction at the same time of day," said Lazarus.

"Well we don't have much choice other than let Hassanein catch our friend before we have a chance, so let's get moving," said Katarina, kicking her donkey on and heading in the tracks of the departed.

"She's a bit of a go-getter, isn't she?" marveled Petrie.

"You have no idea," said Lazarus.

It was the hottest part of the day. While their fellow passengers were no doubt enjoying cool water in the shade of the monuments at Abydus, Lazarus and his companions sweltered under the beating glare of the sun as they journeyed ever southwards.

The sluggish waters of the Nile drifted past in the opposite direction, and no cooling wind stirred the palms and halfeh grass that grew thick on either side of the beaten path. They occasionally passed villagers who naturally plagued them for *baksheesh,* but they didn't have the heart to beat them away with sticks as they saw Captain Hassanein doing in the distance. Soon their canteens were running empty, but at least the sun had begun its descent towards the horizon.

It was dusk by the time they reached the village that was apparently Murad's destination. They only knew this because Captain Hassanein and Émile Brugsch had stopped and were cooling off in the shade several hundred yards short of the first of the buildings. There was no sign of Murad.

"Well I hope you haven't lost him," said Katarina, as they approached them.

They didn't show any surprise at their appearance and had probably known they were being followed the whole time.

"Good lord, is that you, Petrie?" said Brugsch in heavily accented English. "I might have known you'd be outraged enough to join us in our crusade against the thieves should news of their activities reach your ears. Ah, this must be the Russian operative, Miss Mikolavna. A pleasure to meet you, my dear."

Katarina did not acknowledge him. "Where is Murad, Captain?"

"Is that his name?" Hassanein said. "I must thank your friends for handing me this lead. I shall make my appreciation known to both of your governments."

"Drop the small talk, Hassanein," said Lazarus. "Where is he?"

"He wandered into that village up ahead. It is called

Qurna and is one of three such fleapits in this locality. No doubt he meets his contacts here. This part of the country is swarming with tomb robbers."

"So why have you stopped here on the outskirts?"

"You do not realize the situation in our country, Mr. Longman. The difference between city and countryside is even more vast than in England. Many such villages as these do not even consider themselves under the Khedive's rule. Some voiced support for the Mahdist cause in the Soudan. They do not like us city people, the police in particular."

"They're practically savages," said Brugsch. "They've been isolated from the urban centers and beyond the reach of authority for so long that they're more or less independent out here."

"In short, you're scared," said Lazarus.

The captain snorted. "I have a boatload of reinforcements en route. When they arrive, we shall enter the village and begin interrogations."

"And in the meantime, Murad may slip away, along with anybody else of value to us."

"I advise against entering the village, if that's what you are intending, Mr. Longman. If *I* would be putting myself in danger by entering, then it would be near suicide for three Europeans to do so."

"Now see here," said Petrie. "I've entered many such villages in the course of my excavations and although I must admit that there is little to recommend them, I found the people to be generally willing to help in any matter so long as they are dealt with fairly and with respect."

"Yes, but in your expeditions you were always accompanied by guides and hired guards," said Brugsch.

"True…" mused Petrie.

"We do not require armed thugs," said Lazarus. "Isn't that right, Flinders?"

"What? Ah! Oh, yes…"

"Well are we going in or not?" Katarina asked.

"Gentlemen!" exclaimed Brugsch. "I must protest at the suggestion of bringing a lady into such a disease and poverty-stricken hell hole!"

"Are you going to accompany me or stop me, sir?" asked Katarina, her eyes daring the German to pick one of the two.

He lapsed into an embarrassed silence. Katarina turned to face the village. Lazarus led the way and the trio plodded off towards the cluster of mud brick hovels and cone-shaped grain silos that lay partly shaded by sprouting palms.

CHAPTER SEVEN

In which a village fights for its independence

A 'disease and poverty-stricken hell hole' was an apt term for the village. Children capered about in the gutters, some of them with nasty eye infections which drew buzzing hordes of small flies. Haggard men, little more than skeletons, worked away in the irrigated fields and women in their black gowns plastered the houses and washed clothes out on the street. There were none of the water vendors, coffee sellers or shoeshine boys one saw in Cairo; a city that catered and profited from the needs of wealthy travelers. Here, all were engaged in a daily struggle for existence and the mere presence of travelers seemed to be a rare and unwelcome occasion.

"You've noticed that we're being followed?" Petrie asked Lazarus.

Lazarus had indeed become aware of the three young men who had been trailing behind them ever since they entered the village. They seemed to be carrying clubs of some sort.

A woman poked her head out from a nearby window and they saw her eyes widen as she noticed them. She shouted out something in Arabic, but Lazarus wasn't quick enough to make out what she said or if it was directed at them. Somewhere else a window shutter slammed closed and there was the sound of bolts being drawn on the heavy wooden door. It had gone eerily quiet, and Lazarus hadn't even noticed when all the children had vanished. He halted suddenly and muttered under his breath, "To hell with this," and spun around to face the three men following them, his hand passing underneath the left breast of his jacket.

"Is there something we can do for you three?" he asked in Arabic.

They grinned at him and one of them spoke. "We wish to ask you the same question."

"Why have you come to our village?" asked another.

"We're looking for a man," Lazarus explained. "Murad Yasin."

"There is nobody here in Qurna by that name," said the first man.

"He's not from this village but he arrived here moments before we did. We wish to speak with this man."

This seemed to confuse the three men. "Come with us," said one of them.

They were led to one of the larger houses in the village. Most consisted of two rooms; one with a fireplace where the inhabitants shared space with their animals, and one for entertaining guests. This house had several rooms. They were plain and unfurnished, but the mere size of the dwelling hinted that its owners might be slightly better off than their neighbors. Inside, a woman was squatting on the floor kneading bread. A girl of five or six years sat watching her. Somewhere in the rear of the house they could hear the clucking of chickens.

"Sit, please," said one of the men.

They sat down with the three men squatting near

the door.

"My husband will not be home for some time," said the woman through her veil. "Would you care for some water?"

"Yes, please," answered Lazarus.

The woman ordered the girl to fetch it. She returned, struggling with a jug and three cups. They drank the water and watched the woman kneading her bread. The woman eyed them suspiciously, paying special attention to Katarina. When she had finished, she took the bread into the adjoining room and set it to rise by the fire.

"Who is the master of this house?" Lazarus asked one of the three men.

"My cousin, Ahmed," replied one.

"And who is Ahmed?"

"He is a man who commands great respect in Qurna as well as the other villages nearby."

"Like a chief?"

"Yes, like a chief."

"Does he know Murad Yasin?"

There was no reply to this.

"I say, Lazarus," said Petrie. "I don't much like the look of this. Those three are sitting pretty close to the door. It's almost as if we were being held under guard."

"I think that's exactly what's happening," Lazarus replied.

Darkness had fallen outside. The door opened and two men entered. Their khalats were dusty, as if they had been out in the desert all day. They eyed Lazarus and his companions carefully.

"What's all this?" asked the older bearded one. Lazarus guessed this to be Ahmed.

His cousin explained the situation to him.

"I am Ahmed el-Rasoul," said the bearded man, not extending his hand. "This is my brother Mohamed. You three are trespassers here."

"We have no wish to trespass," said Lazarus. "We are seeking a man, Murad Yasin. He came here only hours ago."

"Why are you seeking this man?"

Lazarus chose his next words very carefully. "We wish to purchase items from him. Antiquities."

"There are a hundred antiquity sellers in the streets of Cairo."

"Ah, but these items are, shall we say, a little special."

"Lies. You are working with the police and have been sent here to trick us."

"We're really not working with the police," Lazarus assured him.

"And why would the police be interested in you anyway?" asked Katarina in faulty but coherent Arabic, showing that she had been following the conversation well enough. "Got something to hide?"

"Who is this woman who thinks she can talk to me?" Ahmed asked. "We do not like city people here. And we like tourists even less. And you three stink of wealth and corruption."

He beckoned his brother to follow him into the next room, leaving Lazarus and his companions to sit and stare into the grins of the three youths who guarded the door. Lazarus clicked the joints in the fingers and the wrist of his right hand, his mind on the revolver beneath his breast pocket. If they were going to have to fight their way out of here, he was going to have to draw fast.

There came the sound of arguing from the next

room. Ahmed was shouting his brother down who had apparently stepped out of line.

"Suppose that fellow means to kill us?" Petrie whispered to Lazarus. "And his brother dared to question him? It's nice to have a vote of confidence in a situation like this but I don't fancy his chances of winning the argument. Or ours of getting out of here in one piece."

"Let's not get carried away, Flinders," said Lazarus. "They haven't drawn knives on us yet. And we're all armed, aren't we?"

"What, even Miss Mikolavna?"

"I wouldn't be much of an agent if I only carried a parasol to defend myself with now, would I?" Katarina said.

There came the sound of shouting, but from outside the house this time and from women's throats. Ahmed and Mohamed rushed into the room and peered out into the street. Ahmed turned, his face livid in the lamplight.

"Lying dogs! Did I not say you were lying? Now your police friends are going from door to door, bullying my people and threatening to ransack their homes!"

"Oh, that foolish oaf!" Lazarus hissed. "Couldn't he have waited until we reported back to him?"

Ahmed was shouting orders to the male members of his family who were dragging chests out into the center of the room and flipping the lids open. Martini Henry carbines were produced, and Colt revolvers. The family was turning out to be a regular militia. They filed out into the street and shots were instantly fired. Ahmed slung the six barreled hunk of a Gatling gun over one shoulder and shoved its tripod under the other arm before heading to the steps that led up onto the roof.

"Bloody hell!" Petrie exclaimed.

"That was a Gatling Jericho gun," Lazarus remarked. "And those Colts—American gear."

"No mystery who they got them from," said Katarina. "We're in the right village, at least."

"But at decidedly the wrong time," said Lazarus as the 'boom-boom-boom' of Ahmed's rounds sounded out from the rooftop. "Come on, let's make a break for it."

One of Ahmed's cousins stood in the entrance, blocking their way onto the street, a carbine held across his chest. Mohamed cried out to him, "Let them pass, in the name of Allah! What use are they to us?"

"Shut up and take that chest of ammunition up to your brother, Mohamed!" said the man in the doorway.

Mohamed, cowed once again, did as he was told. An explosion rocked the building and they were thrown off their feet as dust and fragments of shattered mud brick filled the air.

"They're using grenades in a civilian area, the mad bastards!" said Lazarus, coughing on the dust.

He was on his feet before their opponent and drew his revolver in one fluid motion. The man tried to level his rifle at him, but Lazarus sent a bullet into his forehead that knocked him backwards, spilling out a long stream of blood. There were cries from the men in the street who had seen what he had done. Several bullets ricocheted off the wall, forcing Lazarus and his companions to duck. Another explosion lit up the sky as a grenade bounced off the roof of a neighboring building, sending the men in the street hurrying for cover.

"Now's our chance!" said Lazarus, and the three of them were on their feet and hurrying across the debris-strewn street towards the darkness of the palms while the crackle of gunfire sounded out behind them.

Captain Hassanein's men had been forced to retreat during the night, beaten back by the force of the el-Rasoul family's firepower. They sat now in the morning sun by the banks of the Nile, licking their wounds. Lazarus was livid with the police captain, and had told him in no uncertain terms what he thought of a man who stormed a village in the middle of the night without warning and began tossing grenades around.

"And yet you saw the firepower they owned," was the captain's defense. "You see what I have to deal with in my country? Peasants armed with military grade weapons. And who sold them these arms? The British, the French and your American friends."

"Well what are you planning to do now that your police investigation has turned into a war?" asked Katarina. "You've shot to hell any chance of finding the source of the antiquities."

"Not at all," replied Hassanein. "I only need to break their resolve. Once I have worn down their defenses, we shall take the village and every last member of that family shall be bastinadoed until they tell us everything we want to know."

"Well, it looks like they're the ones holding the cane at the moment," said Lazarus.

"Oh, they manage an impressive display of force in street battles," said Hassanein. "But we have the river on our side."

79

"What do you mean?"

"No number of rifles and Gatling guns can stand up to shell bombardment."

Lazarus glanced over the tips of the tents at the military steamer the reinforcements had arrived on last night. Several men on board were uncovering four deck-mounted breechloaders.

"You're not serious," said Lazarus. "You can't blow the place to smithereens and then pick what you want out of the ruins! There's innocents there… women and children!"

"You have seen how innocent they are!" snapped the captain. "Three of my men are dead; men with wives and children! The only answer for villages like these is swift and direct action."

"But at least give them an ultimatum!" Lazarus cried. "Give them a chance to give up what they know before you shell them into oblivion!"

"And risk more of my men's lives by carrying useless messages into that rats' nest?"

"Then I'll go," Lazarus said with determination. "I'll go and speak with this Ahmed el-Rasoul."

"Have you forgotten that you shot and killed one of his cousins?" Katarina asked him. "They'll string you up from the highest palm tree."

"Then I'll go," said Petrie.

They all turned to look at him.

"I'm serious," he said. "They have no reason to despise me. And besides, I have some experience with dealing with villagers like these."

"Good God, man these aren't cheerful fellahs looking for work," broke in Brugsch. "These are desperate rebels with nothing to lose."

"And that is precisely why they might be bargained

with," Petrie replied. "They have no other option but to cooperate to avoid being wiped off the map, if indeed this collection of mud huts exists on any map at all."

"I don't like this, Flinders," said Lazarus. "You're an archeologist and a scholar. It should be an agent like Katarina or myself, someone trained in these situations…"

"Let a woman go in alone while an army of men stand by?" exclaimed Petrie incredulously. "Never, sir!"

Lazarus expected Katarina to put up a fight, not only against Petrie's chivalry but against the whole situation—but she did not. He supposed that even she knew she hadn't a chance of persuading four men to let her wander into the village alone, even if she wanted to.

"Are you sure you can handle this, Flinders?" she said.

"I'm not sure, no," said Petrie. "But I'm the only one here who has a chance of getting everybody out of this situation without any more bloodshed, so I'm bloody well going to try."

They had to agree, and even Captain Hassanein was brought round to the idea, but, he stated, if the scholar did not return by sunset, the bombardment of the village would begin, with him in it if necessary.

They wished the young Egyptologist luck as he handed over his revolver and set off towards the village, his arms raised upwards in a sign of peace. Lazarus was not a praying man but in that moment he offered a silent prayer to any god that might be listening to watch over his friend.

The rest of the day was spent in agonizing waiting.

The police steamer drifted at its mooring threateningly, its guns loaded, manned and ready for action. Captain Hassanein and Émile Brugsch sat smoking in a large tent that had been erected to shade them like some conquering crusaders or Saracens in the time of Richard the Lionhearted.

The sun was beginning to drop and Lazarus couldn't take it anymore. "Listen, Katarina," he said gravely. "If Flinders doesn't meet Hassanein's deadline, I'm going in for him."

"You'll be killed!" said Katarina. "He won't halt the bombardment just because two Englishmen are in there."

"I can't help that, but I asked Flinders along on this mad caper and now he might get killed because of me."

"Didn't you think of that before you invited him along? Didn't you think that it might be dangerous for a scholar to get involved in the things we deal with?"

Her tone was not accusatory, but Lazarus felt accused nonetheless. Poor Flinders had been as eager as anything to accompany him up the Nile. Perhaps he had been blinded to the danger by the thought of what archaeological finds might be out there. Perhaps Lazarus had been blind, too.

Dusk was falling and the shadows were growing deeper. Lights had begun to appear in the village. Torches on the steamer and in the camp also were being lit. The expanse of sand and dust between their encampment and the village looked empty and lonely. Captain Hassanein had left his tent and was stretching his limbs. He was not far away from readying his troops for battle.

"Here he comes!" said Katarina.

Lazarus peered into the gloom. There, by a cluster

of palms, came Petrie hurrying towards them, clearly trying to keep to the shadows. Following him closely was another figure.

"There's somebody with him," pointed out Katarina.

"It's Mohammed," said Lazarus. "The brother who stood up to Ahmed."

Petrie and Mohamed panted into the camp, having run the entire distance from the village. "By God, I'm glad to get out of there!" the Egyptologist exclaimed.

"What happened?" asked Katarina.

"Water first," panted Petrie. "And for my friend Mohamed, also."

"Friend?" demanded Hassanein, his men standing by to clap Mohamed in irons.

"Stay your brutality for five minutes, Captain," said Petrie. "This man came of his own free will and has agreed to help us."

Water was brought and the two men drank deeply.

"The negotiations lasted the whole afternoon," explained Petrie, toweling his face and neck off with a damp cloth. "Ahmed was ready to have me executed as a foreign spy and a minion of the Khedive. Thanks to the protestations of his brother here, I am still alive. That's the second time he's saved our life so I'd be grateful if he was treated gently."

"Why do you stand against your brother to save us?" Lazarus asked Mohamed in Arabic.

"My brother and I have not seen eye to eye in many months," the Egyptian replied. "Since our father died, he has assumed the role as head of the family and yet he still treats me as if I were a child and not a man of twenty-two."

"And for this you betray him?" Captain Hassanein

demanded, clearly not believing a word of it.

"He steals from the family also," said Mohamed, casting his eyes downwards. Lazarus understood that no matter what his brother had done, this betrayal came hard to young Mohammed. "He does not give me my share."

"Share of what?" Hassanein asked. "There's very little wealth to be had in this pit of squalor and yet your family seems to live in a large and well-kept house."

"My share of the money we make from selling treasures."

"So you admit to robbing tombs and selling on their goods?" said Brugsch. "Do you know the location of any tombs that the Antiquities Department is unaware of?"

"Yes," said Mohammed. "There is one tomb, near Deir el-Bahari. I discovered the entrance six years ago. It is a deep one, accessible only via a hole in the ground."

"Six years?" exclaimed Brugsch. "And you've kept it secret all this time?"

"Yes. At first we kept strangers away by killing a donkey and leaving it to foul at the entrance to the tomb. The stink was terrible but it meant that nobody came near. But then, people started to notice our goods on the market and became suspicious, so we stopped selling for a time. Ahmed is a risk taker and driven by greed. It was he who wanted to start selling again. I told him we should wait another year, but he insisted. And now the whole family is in danger because of his greed."

"If this fellow agrees to take us to the tomb," said Petrie, "can we assure him that he will be dealt with leniently or preferably pardoned for his part in the crimes?"

Hassanein grimaced. He clearly would have preferred to get a confession out of Mohamed in his own way, thus avoiding the need to strike a deal, but even the iron-fisted police captain had to see that Mohamed was being surprisingly helpful. "Very well," Hassanein said. "If he continues to help us then I see no reason to press charges. His brother on the other hand…"

"Then we shall set off at first light?" Lazarus asked.

"Yes. For now, get some rest. This prisoner—ah, *witness*—shall be kept under close guard."

Chapter Eight

In which the City of the Silver Aten is discovered

"You do realize that Mohamed was not telling us the whole truth," Petrie said, once Brugsch and Hassanein had retired to their tent and Mohamed had been taken to a secure part of the camp.

"Oh?" said Lazarus.

"Doubtless he knows the location of a royal tomb somewhere in this area, but the silver items probably come from a different source."

"You yourself said that the royal mummies hail from several different dynasties," said Lazarus. "Perhaps they were all moved into a tomb connected with the silver Aten."

"Perhaps, but the tomb Mohamed described sounds like a small one, most likely the tomb of a minor royal figure, or perhaps one of a priest or nobleman simply used as a cache for the other mummies. Lindholm and Rousseau must have found something bigger to spend so much time out here. I'm guessing they have found a religious centre, perhaps as large as Tell el-Amarna, and have employed these villagers to either work there or to ward off snoopers like ourselves by providing them with American arms. And, Mohamed said that this tomb at Deir el-Bahari was discovered six years ago, long before Lindholm came to Egypt."

"I've a feeling you're right," said Lazarus. "I'd like to ask Mohamed a few more questions without Captain Hassanein present."

It was arranged easily enough. There were three men guarding the tent where Mohamed was being kept. Lazarus explained to them that their close proximity might tighten the prisoner's tongue under further interrogations and persuaded them to take a few steps out of earshot. Afforded this little privacy, they put their questions to the Egyptian.

He seemed reluctant at first to betray his family further, but after Lazarus and Petrie had convinced him that they knew a damn sight more than they should about certain things, coupled with their assurances that under no circumstances would the results of this second interrogation reach the ears of Captain Hassanein, Mohamed began to talk.

"It was last year. An American came to our village and talked for a long time with Ahmed. I was not allowed in on the negotiations, but they made a deal about a place buried in the sand further west that we did not know about. I don't know how the American knew of it for none of my people had ever heard of or seen the place."

"This American," said Lazarus, "did he have a woman with him? A lover, perhaps?"

"He had a French woman," said Mohamed. "I do not know if she was his lover."

"All right, go on."

"Ahmed, I and our cousins were employed by this American to dig and to contract people from the other villages to dig at this new site. He paid us well in coin and in supplies; food, materials, weapons. We were to protect the site at all costs and to tell nobody of it under pain of death. Ahmed ensured these rules were adhered to. Three villagers already lie in shallow graves because they broke the rules."

"But these rules did not forbid the taking of items from this new site," said Petrie. "The silver items."

"Ahmed again. We should not have taken objects from the American's dig but my brother's greed knows no boundaries. He would have killed anybody else who might have attempted the same, but he stole the items himself and passed them on to Murad to sell in Cairo. He felt that our original source of treasure was running low after the American began requesting the mummies be removed to his temple complex."

"Wait, the American wanted the mummies removed from Deir el-Bahari?" asked Lazarus.

"Yes, only the mummies. He wasn't interested in the treasure, just the mummies. We took them to him one at a time under cover of night. But there are still many that remain."

"What did he want them for?"

"I don't know. I tried to tell Ahmed that as long as the American did not want our treasure then we did not need to steal from his site, but my brother has grown paranoid over the years and will not let any piece of gold, silver or turquoise slip through his fingers."

"What is this new site like?" Petrie asked him.

"It is an evil place," Mohamed mumbled as if haunted by memories of it. "Big. Many tombs, many temples."

"Hear that?" Petrie hissed to Lazarus in English. "This could make my name in Egyptology!"

"But evil spirits walk those ruins," said Mohamed as if picking up on Petrie's enthusiasm. "Ancient, pagan things from before the birth of the Prophet. The old people destroyed it for a reason, and it should have been left beneath the sand, forgotten."

"The old people destroyed it?" Petrie asked. "Do you mean intentionally razed it to the ground?"

"Yes."

"Just like at Akhetaten…"

"The buildings on the surface are naught but ruins and rubble, but beneath the earth are many caverns left untouched—secret places that even the old people did not find. My own people refused to go down there after we had broken the seal. Only the American and his woman dared to."

"Are you telling me that the seal was unbroken when you uncovered the city?" asked Petrie with great excitement.

"Yes."

"Does this American and his woman live up at the site?" Lazarus asked.

"Yes. There are a handful of my people who camp there also as guards, but they do not go down into the tombs. Only the American and his woman. What they do down there I do not know, nor do I wish to."

"Where is this place? Tell us how to get there."

"You must travel west, keeping between the two mountain peaks. Once you are on the other side of them, turn south, following the wall of the canyon. When that wall sinks down into sand, continue west and then, after half a day you will find the ruined city."

Feeling that there was no more to be got from the Egyptian, they retired and held a council on what was to be done.

"On the morrow, Petrie," Lazarus said, "Émile Brugsch will make a discovery the like of which has never been seen before—a cache of royal mummies spanning many dynasties. Are you sure you want to let him have all the glory by throwing your lot in with us?"

"Lazarus, my friend, there is no question of it. We shall make a discovery that will eclipse any moldy old mummies that Brugsch might find. If what I believe is correct, then we shall find another Akhetaten! The twin of Akhenaten's religious metropolis! The home of the second half of his heretical faith!"

"Very good. And you, Katarina? You haven't shot me yet, so I suppose we're still friends."

"Your best bet at staying friends with me, Longman, is to stay out of my way when we reach this desert city. Lindholm is mine, do not forget that."

Lazarus sighed and they began kitting themselves out for a long journey. At daybreak they pinched three camels from the soldiers and enough durra grain to feed them for three days. While Captain Hassanein and the rest of the camp were still slumbering by the river, they loaded the camels up with full canteens and as much spare food as they could pilfer from the camp's stores. They set out before sunrise, following the river south, breaking off towards the mountains as the sun was just beginning to creep up over the horizon at their backs; Akhenaten's god, leering at them, daring them to find his twin out in the desert.

They slept during the hottest part of the day, shaded by some rocks, before setting out again after the sun had passed overhead. The night was cold and by the time they had passed through the shaded valley between the mountains, they were chilled to the bone.

The next day, at last, across the vast plains, they could make out a scarred patch in the land where sand had recently been cleared away and mounded up in piles around it. A small encampment had been erected and the smoke and faint light of campfires could be made out in the fading light.

"How can this place remain a secret?" asked Katarina. "It's just sitting here for anybody to stumble over it."

"Few people venture this far into the barren wilderness," said Petrie.

Lazarus had to admit that it truly felt like the ends of the earth out here, and he wondered if it had been Akhenaten's plan to build a city so far beyond the borders of civilization. But then, the Silver Aten was the flipside of the sun. If the Aten symbolized life, then surely the Silver Aten meant death. It would make sense to build its temples far away from the hustle and bustle of Akhetaten—the city of the sun and of light and life.

They left the camels and proceeded on foot under the cover of the coming darkness. They skirted the camp and came upon the ruins from the south. They did not want to draw the attention of any guards that might be lurking about, but even from a distance they could make out some remarkable details. A large canvas covered a bulky shape, but Lazarus and Katarina could make out what it was at once.

"He's got a bloody airship!" said Lazarus. "One of those small Confederate jobs like the *Santa Bella*."

"Not mechanite-powered, surely?" said Petrie.

"Not unless he's smuggled some out of the C.S.A. No, it's most likely one of the early coal-burning ones. Must come in handy for scouting the landscape, not to mention shipping in supplies."

There was also many steam-powered digging machines; state of the art pieces that could shift large masses of dirt without the need to pay twenty fellahs to do it with shovels. These in particular had Petrie in a state of excitement.

"Where does he get the money for these things? I haven't even seen some of this stuff and I'm an established archaeologist! I only hope he didn't dig too deep and damage something. I still maintain that the only way to effectively remove large amounts of surface sand and dirt is by hand, even if it takes fifty men a whole week. It's the only safe way to uncover the first strata."

"Let's keep our voices down," said Katarina. "We're drawing close now. Have your weapons ready. It looks like they've got gas lamps rigged up."

Hands resting on revolvers, they entered the outskirts of the city, keeping to the shadows and avoiding the gas lamps hanging from tripods and strapped to crumbling pillars.

"I think we just passed the first pylon," said Petrie, referring to the twin structures that usually straddled the pathway into any city or religious centre.

"I didn't see anything," remarked Katarina.

"There's not much to see but to the eye of a trained archaeologist," said Lazarus. "Those flattened squares of stone over there once rose up several hundred feet, like the towers of a fortress. There'll be another pair further to our left. We're not entering the city through its main gates, you see, but from the south."

"How can you tell?"

"It makes sense for the gates to the city of the setting sun—or death if you prefer—to face the rising sun, ready to swallow it as it descends. This is where the sun comes to die."

"City of death," murmured Katarina, glancing

around at the shattered blocks of stone and the deep shadows. "Wonderful."

As Lazarus had predicted, they passed between the second pylon by turning left and following a broken pavement deeper into the ruins. Some lights up ahead bounced off the surfaces of a large mound of earth, recently excavated. They could make out the silhouettes of several men in khalats guarding a stairway that led down into the earth.

"That must be the entrance to the underground section Mohamed mentioned," said Petrie. "Where the seal was found intact!" He was clearly excited, and Lazarus was worried that he might not be able to keep his voice down. By the light of the lamps he could see that the men up ahead had rifles. Now was not the time to let their scholarly pursuits carry them away.

"How are we going to get down there and get Lindholm out?" Katarina said. "There's too many men in and around this place to use force."

"There's something that strikes me as odd about this whole place," said Lazarus. "Usually temples to the Aten are wide open spaces, like at Akhetaten. This place seems to keep its most sacred places covered up, like the temples to older Egyptian deities."

"Think about it, Lazarus," said Petrie. "If worship of the sun took place out in the open, where its light could fill every nook and cranny, where would worship of the moon take place?"

"Underground, of course," said Lazarus. "But the light of the moon must be let in somehow."

"Correct. It must be channeled in through small apertures. We know the Egyptians used mirrors to direct light. Perhaps they caught the sheen of the moon and used it to illuminate their underground temples."

Lazarus glanced up at the darkening sky. There was no moon yet. "How do we find it?"

"I'm guessing Lindholm and Rousseau already have. They would have seen the opening from below when they were exploring the chambers. If the aperture was blocked, they would have certainly unblocked it. It shouldn't be too hard to find."

They wandered deeper into the crumbling remains, searching the ground for holes. Katarina spotted a pile of supplies and earth and, after investigating, called the other two over. "Is this what we're looking for?" she asked.

They peered down the hole. Nothing but blackness yawned before them.

"This must be it," said Petrie, uncoiling the rope from his satchel. "Get ready to lower me down."

"Hold on a minute," said Lazarus. "We don't know what's down there."

"Oh, come on, Lazarus," said Petrie, fastening the rope around his waist. "All the guards are either sleeping or loitering around the entrance. And you heard Mohammed say that only Lindholm and Rousseau dare to go down below. Or is it the evil spirits you are afraid of?"

"Very well," said Lazarus, pursing his lips at his friend's sarcasm. "Just have your revolver ready should anything happen down there. What about light?"

"You'll have to pass down a lamp once I reach the bottom. I don't have a free hand."

Lazarus began lowering Petrie while Katarina unpacked a lamp and got it lit, shielding it with her satchel so that the glare would not be noticed from the other end of the city. Lazarus grimaced as the form of his friend was swallowed by the blackness. The rope

95

suddenly went slack.

Petrie's voice called up from the chamber, closer than Lazarus had anticipated. "Send down the lamp, quickly! I can't see a blessed thing down here!"

Lazarus hauled up the rope and tied the lamp to it before lowering it back down. They waited while Petrie made his preliminary investigations of whatever room they had dropped him into.

"Get down here, you two!" he called up at last. "This is fabulous!"

After some bickering about who was going to lower whom, Lazarus let Katarina down into the chamber, and then fastened the rope around the base of a pillar and climbed down, wincing at the burning of his palms as he slipped a few feet.

He found himself in a wide chamber the corners of which could not be illuminated all at once by Petrie's lamp. They stood in a basin that looked like it had been built to contain water. A block stood in the centre of it with a hole in the middle that had been used to receive a pole of some sort, probably the polished bronze mirror that had been used to direct the light of the moon. Petrie was over by the far wall examining the paintings and the hieroglyphics with acute interest. Lazarus joined him.

"Magnificent!" Petrie was saying, over and over again. "Look at the style! It's Amarna period to a tee!"

Lazarus could indeed make out the images of Akhenaten and Nefertiti and their children in the distinctive realist style of their reign. The crescent disc of the moon hovered above, shining down its rays, just as images of the sun did at Akhetaten. But whereas those rays often ended in little hands or ankhs symbolizing the life given by the sun, these rays of the moon ended in the symbol of the *amenta*, representing the western horizon and the taking away of life. "If there was ever proof needed that we are in the city of death, then this is it," remarked Lazarus.

"Can you two drop your scholarly interest for once and think about what we're here to do?" said Katarina, showing uncharacteristic nervousness.

"Actually this is what I'm here to do," said Petrie. "But I suppose my job will be easier if you two get rid of that American fellow and Mademoiselle Rousseau. Here's a doorway, my goodness, it goes off in two directions. Which to take?"

"It's probably a bloody maze down here," said Lazarus, peering down each of the dark corridors. "What's the plan? Split up?"

"Of all the stupidest ideas you've had since I met you, Longman," growled Katarina, "that is the worst."

"Surely you're not scared down here, Katarina?" Lazarus asked, knowing that she could make out the grin on his face even in the dim light. "You have two strong men here to protect you."

Katarina's face turned to one of rage as she snatched the lamp from Petrie and headed off down the left corridor, her pistol cocked and held out, ready to shoot anything that got in her way.

"Well, at least she's not pointing it at me for a change," Lazarus mumbled.

CHAPTER NINE

In which the experiments of Dr. Lindholm are revealed

Lazarus was reminded, with a certain degree of trepidation, of the labyrinthine tunnels beneath the lake in Arizona that connected the seven golden cities of Cibola. But whereas those tunnels were rough and hewn from the living rock, these were lined with well-cut bricks which made every turn sharp and angular. They passed through a series of rooms, richly decorated and clearly used for priestly functions. Nowhere were there images of deities common in other Egyptian temples—Anubis, Hathor, Osiris and Ra—only the image of the moon and its rays, bouncing off the walls in geometric lines.

"Stop!" hissed Lazarus, grabbing Petrie and motioning Katarina to halt her steady march into the unknown.

"What is it?" she demanded, holding the lamp up to his face. As she did so, she became suddenly aware that she no longer needed it. Lamps had been set up at regular intervals down the corridors.

"I think we're nearing the viper's lair," Lazarus said. "Proceed carefully."

There came a sound from the far end of a corridor that branched off to the right. It was a kind of scuffling, stomping sound, not slow, but fast and juddering.

Lazarus was sure he was not the only one who was put in mind of a giant beetle scuttling down the passageway towards them.

The corridor was cloaked in blackness, but the three of them became very aware of a threat edging closer and closer. There was a slow hissing, as of a snake, that galvanized the trio into action, sending them fleeing in the opposite direction. Whatever was coming towards them, they did not want to wait and find out if bullets could harm it.

They took passages at random, hoping to throw whatever it was that was following them off their scent, and eventually emerged in what appeared to be a dead end.

"We're trapped!" said Katarina.

"Wait a minute," said Petrie, forgetting his fear for a moment. "What's this?"

There was a sarcophagus in the center of the room, surrounded by silver ushabtis that were set out like a toy army at its feet. The lid, if the sarcophagus ever had one, had been removed. There was an open coffin within, also lidless, containing a mummy. It was a sad, shriveled brown thing with a silver mask fashioned in the features of a woman.

"Now who can this be?" said Petrie, approaching the sarcophagus.

"For God's sake, man, this is no time to be examining mummies!" said Katarina.

Indeed, the shuffling sound was approaching the chamber, growing closer and closer.

"Now we're for it!" said Lazarus. "Get ready to open fire. You too Petrie!"

But Petrie wasn't listening. He was crouched by the sarcophagus examining the hieroglyphics inscribed on its sides. "This is fabulous! Do you know who this is?"

"No one cares, Petrie!" Lazarus shouted, the footsteps very close now.

"This is Kiya! The very same woman whose kohl container I found at Akhetaten. This is her mummy right here!"

"Really?" asked Lazarus, momentarily interested.

"God, not you too!" shouted Katarina. "Keep your eyes on that doorway, Longman, and your mind on shooting whatever comes through it!"

"Right! Sorry."

A shape emerged from the gloom. Both Lazarus and Katarina raised their pistols and put their fingers on the triggers, but halted just in time.

"Oh, please don't shoot me!" cried a woman's voice.

As the figure moved into the light, Lazarus instinctively lowered his weapon. Katarina kept hers trained on the woman, not trusting anything or anyone right now.

"I heard voices and was intrigued," said the woman. "Tell me, how did you three come to be down here?"

She was beautiful, and her voice hinted at exotic parts. Her hair was black and fell loosely over slender shoulders. Her dress was not so different to Katarina's, being attire suited to a female in rugged terrain, and as in Katarina's case, this was in no way unflattering. But it was her eyes that caught Lazarus's attention. They were dark and heavy-lidded, a smoky hazel color.

"Mademoiselle Rousseau?" Lazarus hazarded.

"Yes," she replied. "And yes, that is indeed Kiya in the sarcophagus, poor woman."

"Mmm?" answered Petrie who had not even turned around to take note of the newcomer, so infatuated he was with his discovery. "Oh? Yes. Fascinating! Fascinating!" He then seemed to remember himself and spun around before bowing low. "Mademoiselle Rousseau, it is an honor to finally meet you. Your work at KV55 had me green with envy, positively green. It is a great pleasure to finally make your acquaintance."

Eleanor Rousseau seemed amused by the young man and smiled. "The honor is mine, Mr. Petrie."

"Oh? Ah! You seem to know me… but how?"

"Your stupendous work on the pyramids at Gizah has ensured your immortality amongst us Egyptologists," she replied. "And your excavations at Akhetaten have captured my heart for that place is so dear to me."

"My dear," said Petrie, "your work in uncovering this city of the moon has far surpassed anything I have done or could ever hope to achieve."

"But I am unacquainted with your two associates," said Rousseau.

"Allow me to introduce them! This is my good friend Lazarus Longman, a fellow Englishman and fellow Egyptologist, although that is but one of his many areas of expertise. And this is Miss Katarina Mikolavna, a Russian traveler who is a friend of Longman's."

"Charmed to meet you both," said Rousseau.

"Likewise," said Katarina without a smile. Lazarus instantly detected the tension in the Russian. He knew Katarina far too well to hope that she might get on with the likes of Eleanor Rousseau.

"But what on earth are you all doing down here?" Rousseau asked. "Don't you know that this area is off limits to everybody but those Dr. Lindholm gives special permission to?"

"As Dr. Lindholm has not even applied for a concession with the Antiquities Department," Petrie said, "I find it a bit much that he forbids anybody else to come here. And those fellahs guarding the entrance! What is he doing here, raising his own private army?"

"You have no idea how close you are to the truth in saying that," she replied. "He is truly a monster. But you must go! Immediately! Your lives are in the greatest peril!"

"Very well," said Lazarus. "But you are coming with us."

"I cannot," said Rousseau. "My work here is too important."

"But you just said that Lindholm is a monster," said Lazarus.

"Even so, he will not hurt me. He needs my knowledge, and I must remain to ensure the safe removal of Kiya and the other artifacts in this tomb."

"You do not understand the situation," said Lazarus. "I am acquainted with your husband, Henry. We worked together for the Royal Archaeological Society when we were younger. We did not part on the best of terms but that is no longer relevant. I have since been employed by Her Majesty's government as an agent. My mission is to bring you safely home."

"What?" he heard Katarina exclaim behind him. "You're here for her?"

He ignored her. "Please, Eleanor, see that you must come with me. We'll let the Russians deal with Lindholm. Katarina here is under the Tsar's orders. Once he is gone I am sure you can return here and continue your work, free from all this danger and secrecy."

"You are sweet, Mr. Longman," Eleanor replied.

"But I fear that it is you who does not understand the situation."

She did not say any more, for they could all hear the shuffling, stomping sound they had heard before, rustling, scraping and hissing as it came closer and closer.

"For God's sake, go, all of you!" said Eleanor. "Don't let it trap you in here!"

"What is it?" Lazarus asked her.

"One of Lindholm's creations."

"I won't leave you here with it."

"It won't harm me, but it will tear you three apart!"

"Even if we flee now, I'll still come back for you, Eleanor. That's my mission and by God, I'm going to fulfill it."

"You mustn't come back! Lindholm occasionally lets me come into Cairo to organize supplies and deliver paperwork. I can meet you if you like and we can discuss things further. Where are you staying?"

"Longman, we need to get moving!" warned Katarina, her revolver pointed at the darkness from which the sounds were coming.

"Shepheard's Hotel. Look, I really don't…"

"Now, Longman!"

"I think we'd better go," agreed Petrie.

"Cairo, then," said Lazarus to Eleanor by way of parting, and they headed out into the corridor.

Katarina's gun spoke out twice, filling the hallways with a deafening sound and lighting them up with brief orange flares. In those short bursts of light, they finally saw the thing that was advancing on them.

It was tall—taller than a man, but clearly not a man. It had parts of a man, and from the yellowed bandages and brown, shriveled flesh, Lazarus knew exactly where Lindholm had got those parts. One leg was a bandaged spindly thing, but the other was a mass of gears and pistons that elicited the occasional jet of hot steam. Its arms were mechanical too, ending in viciously serrated pincers like those of a giant crab, and powered by pistons that looked like they could crush a man's skull with ease. Two things in the bandaged abdomen of the creature stood out in the darkness. One was where the heart should be, but was a glass orb filled with a misty greenish vapor fitted into a brass grommet. The other was the furnace below its ribcage that heated the boiler it no doubt carried on its back. Lazarus knew this, for he had encountered similar creatures in America. And like those, this one's furnace glowed with the purple light of burning mechanite.

They opened fire on the creature. Bullets pinged off metal surfaces, some thudding into the mummified flesh and when those did not halt the creature, Lazarus understood why Lindholm had become so fascinated with Egypt.

"We can't kill it!" he shouted. "Just get out of here! Run!"

They stopped firing, turned, and pounded down the hallway, not knowing where it might lead them. The creature stomped after them, one metal leg thudding down into the sand and one mummified leg shuffling along to catch up.

They skidded around a corner and dived down a flight of carven steps, to find themselves in another tomb, or at least what had originally been a tomb. It had recently been converted into a workshop of sorts. Trestle tables had been set up and every surface was littered with tools, gadgets and partially completed tinkerings; arms, pincers and joints fashioned in brass which caught the light of the gas lamps, their oily surfaces glittering like gold.

It was then that they noticed the moving things. In every corner there lurked a creature—small, but beetling about like oversized cockroaches. They pointed their guns in all directions, each of them trying to assess where the greatest threat lay.

"They're just animals," said Katarina. "Not dangerous."

Indeed they were animals, or had been once. There were two mummified cats with their hindquarters replaced by mechanics dozing on a workbench, while a jackal nosed around under a table, futilely sniffing the ground through its bandaged nostrils. A bird of some sort flapped its metal wings on its perch high up near the ceiling. Each of them had the miniature boiler and mechanite furnace, as well as the green orb enclosing the heart, no bigger than golf balls in the cat's cases.

"Lindholm's experiments?" said Lazarus.

"How on earth has he reanimated the dead?" Katarina asked.

"It's like he is the Modern Prometheus from Shelly's *Frankenstein*," murmured Petrie.

"I'm not one for believing in magic," said Lazarus, "even the ancient Egyptian kind, but I just don't see how science, even the mad science of Dr. Lindholm could have achieved this."

"Maybe it's a combination of both," said Petrie. "The ancient Egyptians believed that the soul resided in the heart, not the brain. That is why the heart was the only organ left in the body during mummification. All of these creatures seem to have some gadget fitted around the heart. I don't pretend to understand it, but there it is."

"But the brain," said Lazarus, unconvinced, "the nervous system…"

"It's found us!" said Katarina.

They could hear it coming, clanking down the steps that led into the workshop. They scurried for cover, diving behind tables. Lazarus shooed away the jackal which looked at him dejectedly, then loped off to find something else to sniff at.

The mechanical monster stomped into the room and halted. It looked around with blind eye sockets, its bandaged head craning forward as if sniffing them out. Lazarus rose up and leveled his pistol at the green orb in the creature's chest. He squeezed the trigger and sent a bullet smashing through the glass. It exploded in a shower of splinters. He had expected, perhaps, a cloud of the green vapor to escape, but it was liquid that trickled forth; green and sluggish like blood of the wrong color.

The creature looked down at its ruptured chest, then touched the green substance that soaked its bandages and ran down its mechanical leg in rivulets. Its face seemed to look confused, or as near as was possible for a three thousand year old mummified face to express any emotion. It stumbled backwards, its mummified leg giving out. It toppled over and crashed to the stone floor to lay motionless, steam jetting out from its still functioning mechanics like the soul escaping the corpse of the deceased.

"Thank God they can be killed," said Katarina rising.

"As long as you aim for the heart, it seems," said Lazarus.

They headed back up the steps and out into the passageway.

"More of them," said Petrie, pointing down the hallway.

Two of the beasts were shambling through the shadows on the scent of those who had killed one of their number. One of them was a twin for the first mechanical mummy—a human, perhaps a priest or even a pharaoh, revived after three thousand years and assimilated into a mechanical locomotive—but the other had the fore section of a human and the hindquarters of an enormous mechanical jackal. There seemed to be no reason for this other than wild experimentation. The powerful back legs sprung the creature forward in great bounds, such as those a tiger or panther might, carrying the groping, bandaged fore section towards them at an alarming rate.

"Where the hell is the exit?" panted Petrie, struggling to keep up with Lazarus and Katarina.

"We won't make it up the rope without one of those blasted things tearing off our legs," said Lazarus. "We'll have to find the real door."

"What makes you think it won't still be guarded?" said Katarina.

"Nothing. But I fancy our chances against some sleepy fools with rifles better than against these things."

"Well maybe one of you two Egyptologists can figure out in what direction the door lies," said Katarina as they rounded a corner and continued down a passage that looked just like the previous one. "This place is just a maze to me."

They entered a chamber that had a deep trench dug into the floor, barely narrow enough for them to cross.

"We must be close," said Petrie. "Such trenches were dug near the entrances of tombs to deter grave robbers."

Katarina made an impressive bound and landed on the other side of the trench in a billow of skirts. The creatures rounded the corner and advanced.

"Toss me your gun and make the jump!" Lazarus shouted to Petrie. "I'll hold them off!"

The Egyptologist did as he was told and leapt across the pit, grabbing Katarina's outstretched arm for support. A gun in each hand, Lazarus fired round after round at the beasts, knowing he was unlikely to hit their hearts at this range but giving it all he had regardless. The bullets did nothing to slow their pace and when the chambers clicked empty, Lazarus turned and bolted towards the trench. He leapt and landed on the opposite side, but was unbalanced and began to topple backwards. With a pistol in each hand, he was unable to grab either Katarina's or Petrie's hands and it was only by seizing his jacket lapels that his companions stopped him from tumbling down into the pit.

There was a whoosh of air behind his ears, followed by a loud 'chomp!' Lazarus was horribly aware that something had leapt up out of the pit to take a bite at him. He craned his head around and looked down. The floor beneath him seemed to be moving. Mechanical beasts of the mummified variety were squirming and rolling about, limbs thrashing and steam billowing up in clouds as they leapt and tried to scale the walls, slipping and sliding back down.

"Amazing!" cried Petrie. "Steam-powered crocodiles!"

"Will you shut up and pull me in, Petrie!" Lazarus yelled.

Katarina and Petrie hauled him towards them and

he staggered forward, glad to have his balance back again. But the creatures behind them were edging towards the pit and they all knew that the one with the jackal legs would certainly be able to make the jump. They continued their flight and found themselves running up steps towards a small rectangle of blue light.

"Here," said Lazarus, tossing Petrie his gun back. "Reload. We're almost out of here."

Sliding cartridges into place as they ran, they ascended the steps and felt the warm desert air in their nostrils. A figure's head and torso blocked the light of the exit and the shape of his rifle was visible. Lazarus fired as he ran, knocking the man back with a cry.

They burst out of the entrance to the underground complex and immediately heard the crack of rifles. They ducked and slid behind cover in the form of crates and piles of earth. Bullets zinged and thudded all around them. Lazarus kept his eye on the doorway, knowing it was only a matter of time before those things would be out and upon them.

There came a cry as the guards heard the sounds of their approaching pursuers from within the doorway. With a bound, the jackal-man barreled out into the light of day and the guards wailed in terror, focusing their fire on the beast.

Seizing their chance, Lazarus and his companions were on their feet and running through the ruins, leaping over fallen columns, heading for the city's outskirts at a breakneck pace. The rest of the Egyptians in the camp were running to the aid of their comrades at the entrance to the catacombs and didn't pay any attention to the three figures fleeing the city. They did not stop running until they felt the sand of the desert under their feet.

CHAPTER TEN

In which further arrangements are made back in Cairo

It was early morning. The sky in the east was turning a pale shade of lavender. They headed towards it, dog tired and with nerves frayed beyond bearing. Nevertheless, Katarina was in the mood for a fight.

"So, Longman, you didn't think to tell me that you weren't really after Dr. Lindholm at all, but his hussy?" she said with a sideways sneer.

"What difference does it make to you which one I was after?" Lazarus replied, too tired for this.

"Not a jot. I just think you could have said something. Why the secrecy? And what on earth do you want her for?"

"She's the fiancé of Henry Thackeray, a very important fellow in London. When news came through that she appeared to have run off with an American, it became a priority to track her down and return her to Britain."

"So all of this—infiltrating the black market, travelling up the Nile, nearly getting yourself killed in that ancient city back there—all this was for the sake of a woman?"

"You make it sound as if I'm pursuing her for my own pleasure. I have a job to do, Katarina, just as you do. If Whitehall decides that I'm to chase after some

113

bloody politician's lady-friend, then that is what I must do."

"And this from a man who once went rogue in America," she spat. "What happened to you, Longman? Why did you return to the service of a country you hate?"

"Let's get one thing straight, Mikolavna, I don't hate my country. There are plenty of things about it that I love."

"And plenty of things you despise."

"I thought she was rather pretty," broke in Petrie. "Rousseau, that is. Very exotic looking. Dark for a French woman. I suppose that's the Mediterranean blood. Dark and sensuous."

"Yes, she was rather something," Lazarus agreed.

Katarina sniffed. "I thought she was rather plain, myself."

The stink of the city was a welcome fragrance to the three weary travelers returning from the desert. It had taken them days to reach the Nile and find passage on a steamer returning to the capital. Lazarus was glad to hear the noise of the vendors and feel the jostle of civilization, after so nearly perishing in lonely tombs and dying of thirst in the burning desert.

They gorged themselves on meat, bread and dates in the marketplace before returning to their respective hotels where they took long baths and slept the sleep of the dead for a whole day.

The following day they met for dinner in the restaurant Lazarus and Petrie had first dined in. Cairo had changed since they had been away. Reaction to

Brugsch's discovery of the Deir el-Bahari cache of royal mummies was a sensation in the city. The newspapers were full of the astonishing find. Over a hundred mummies in total had been stored in the tomb, including Seti I, and most exciting of all, the long sought after remains of Ramses the Great.

Petrie had been right. The mummies had been stored in the tomb of a minor priest to protect them from grave robbers. Tomb robbing being no new profession, they had probably been removed from their own tombs in the Valley of the Kings by priests, way back in antiquity.

There was a feeling of jubilation amongst the denizens of Cairo which surprised Lazarus for a population mostly made up of Mohammedans who often poured scorn on the pagan past of their country. But the lost pharaohs had been found, and although Brugsch had tried to keep the arrival of the mummies in Cairo a secret until they could safely reach the Bulaq museum, the city had got wind of the exciting procession and had poured out onto the streets to welcome the returning pharaohs.

Petrie had devoured the newspaper articles with acute interest and not without a tinge of jealousy. After all, Brugsch had made the discovery of the century, while he had only narrowly escaped death with nothing to show for it.

"Apparently the women of Qurna came out of their homes when Brugsch was leading the mummies down to the riverbanks," Lazarus said over dinner. "Wailing and lamenting the removal of the pharaohs from their resting place. Quite poignant, really."

"Lamenting the removal of their source of income, most likely," said Katarina.

"Must you be so cynical?" Lazarus asked her.

"My, my, you are quite the romantic, aren't you, Longman," she replied. "Who would have thought it of an Englishman?"

"I may as well have donned my mourning veil and joined them," said Petrie, swilling his claret around in his glass melancholically.

"Come now, Flinders, I've already apologized for leading you away on that mad chase instead of leaving you to join in the discovery of the royal cache."

"Oh, it isn't your fault, Lazarus," said Petrie. "I made the decision to come along and I can't say that I regret it, for I saw with my own eyes a lost city that has such importance to our understanding of Akhenaten's reign. It's just tragic that I can never return there without some sort of army at my back."

"Speaking of which," said Katarina in a sour tone, "there isn't a hope in hell of any of us getting back there, which means failure for our respective missions."

"Didn't Rousseau say she would come to Cairo and meet you, Lazarus?" Petrie asked. "What's to stop you from just grabbing her and returning her to England?"

"I can't very well nab the girl off the street," said Lazarus. "For one thing the Egyptian police would have me in irons quicker than you can say 'kidnapping'."

"So this is the stuff British agents are made of," said Katarina with a roll of her eyes. "What exactly was your plan—sweet talk her into coming back with you? Suppose she's quite happy here in the company of Dr. Lindholm?"

"I don't believe that," said Lazarus firmly. "She is not in love with him. You heard her call him a monster.

She's terrified of him, so much so that she dares not run from him."

"And all she needs is a knight in shining armor to rescue her," said Katarina. "You've got it all figured out, haven't you, Romeo?"

The next day, as if summoned by their words the night before, Eleanor Rousseau came to Shepheard's Hotel looking for Lazarus. He found her in reception. She looked even more beautiful bathed in the daylight streaming in from the doors than she had down in the dusky, lamp-lit tombs. She wore a skirt in the Parisian fashion, with a high-shouldered bodice in sky blue. Her hair was perfect. Not for the first time, Lazarus wondered what on earth she saw in Henry Thackeray.

"Hello, Mr. Longman," she said as he approached.

"Call me Lazarus, please. Did you come alone?"

"Apart from the servants Dr. Lindholm always insists I take with me, yes."

"Then we can make our arrangements to return you to England. To Henry."

Her eyes looked down at the marble floor. "It's not as simple as all that. Is there somewhere we might go and talk?"

"Why don't we take the air in Azbekya Gardens?"

"Perfect."

They left the hotel and crossed the street towards the iron gates leading in to the gardens. The morning breeze was refreshingly cool, and the leaves in the tamarisk trees danced gently.

"I wish I could spend more time in Cairo," Eleanor said. "It is so very beautiful. I love my work, but sometimes one grows tired of spending more time with the dead than with the living. I begin to yearn for green things and the sounds of lively cities."

"I know those feelings well," said Lazarus. "I spent much of my youth in tombs and forgotten cities. Although, in recent years I have found myself wishing I had remained an antiquarian. The dead do not present nearly as many problems as the living. At least I thought so until I encountered your American friend's creations."

"Yes, they are quite abominable. But they do not interfere with my work, which is something. Lindholm and I have a mutual understanding for each other's work."

"The paintings I saw in the tomb of Kiya looked spectacularly intriguing," said Lazarus. "Petrie and I would relish a chance to spend some time examining them in closer detail without steam-powered mummies trying to unscrew our heads."

"Unlikely at present," said Eleanor. "You risked far too much in one visit to the City of the Silver Aten that your luck is surely used up. Another attempt would be fatal."

"I fear so. But Petrie in particular envies you your time and proximity to the site. This Kiya woman for example. What's her story?"

Eleanor studied him closely, as if trying to ascertain if he was really interested or merely making polite conversation. She decided on the former. "Yes, I have been making extensive examinations of the tomb of Kiya in particular. Kiya was a priestess of the Aten. She was a woman of formidable power before Akhenaten's religious reforms. In fact, it was she who had such an influence over him that he converted to the worship of the Aten, and it was her suggestion that he build both Akhetaten and the City of the Silver Aten, the original name of which is now lost to us. He made her the High Priestess. They were lovers, you see, and he took her as his wife."

"He married a powerful priestess of another cult?" interrupted Lazarus. "I can't imagine that went down well with Nefertiti!"

"Not at all. The Great Royal Wife was always a jealous bitch, and she hated Kiya from the beginning. Nefertiti's devotion to the Aten extended only as far as her compliance with her husband's demands. She was never a true follower, but was always power hungry and could never suffer another woman to exert such control over her husband. So, the pharaoh and his family moved their court to Akhetaten in the fifth year of his reign. Tension between the Great Royal Wife and Kiya had always been high, and it broke when Kiya bore the pharaoh a son—something Nefertiti had been unable to do, despite the six daughters she had given him. The Queen was enraged and put into motion her vengeance against Kiya.

"Kiya was still recovering on her birthing bed when she struck. With lies to her husband of Kiya's treachery, Nefertiti planted the seed of doubt in Akhenaten's mind. Kiya's newborn son was snatched from her arms and taken away, never to be seen again. The midwives claimed the child had been sickly and had died of natural causes more or less instantly, but Kiya knew better. She knew that the Queen would never allow the pharaoh's son by another woman to grow up in the royal court.

"Kiya was banished. Driven near mad by the loss of her son and swearing vengeance on Nefertiti, she wandered back to her own people. Every instance of her name was stricken from Akhetaten. Her sarcophagus and canopic jars—which had been prepared for her in her lifetime—were used for others, altered to show the names of other members of the royal family. Even to speak her name became a punishable offence.

"After the High Priestess of the Aten was gone from Akhetaten, the new religion began to fall apart. People started to lose their faith in both the Aten and their pharaoh. Discontent grew between the priesthood and the army who were neglected and restless. Trade began to drop off. Corruption was rife. The royal court only remained at the city for four years after Akhenaten's death before moving back to Thebes. Within fifteen years the Horizon of the Aten was a ruined city left to the scorpions and the ghosts. Akhenaten's descendants even moved his body and all the other royal mummies from their tombs to the Valley of the Kings, which is where I found the heretic pharaoh's tomb. Worship of the Aten became a heresy, and statues and temples were defaced or torn down.

"As for Kiya, she died cursing Nefertiti and wailing for her lost son. Her family—who were now members of an underground sect—secretly buried her at the City of the Silver Aten so that the High Priestess would forever reside in the city of her god, even though her restless spirit was barred from the afterlife, her name stolen from her."

"Perhaps her spirit haunts those ruins along with Lindholm's abominations," said Lazarus. "I wonder what she would have to say to them should their paths ever cross."

"I cannot say that I have run into her myself,"

120

Eleanor replied with a ghost of a smile.

"Well, somebody in Cairo is interested in Kiya's tale other than Petrie and I," said Lazarus. "Did you hear about the fragment that was stolen from the Bulaq Museum?"

"Yes, why? Did that have something to do with Kiya?"

"Petrie believes so. He found a kohl container at Akhetaten bearing Kiya's name and thinks the scraped-off hieroglyphics on the fragment is a match."

"It's possible. Kiya's name and image were all over both cities during her time as High Priestess. And no matter how hard her enemies tried, they could never fully erase her memory."

"And now you have found her very tomb containing her remains," said Lazarus. "What will you do next? Something tells me that Dr. Lindholm isn't interested in Ancient Egypt beyond what it can offer his country's diabolical war machine."

"He is no antiquarian, that I can say with certainty," she replied. "It has only been at my insistence that Kiya's mummy be spared the disrespectful mutilations of his experiments. I was so enthralled by her story that I felt a bond to her, which makes me very protective of her remains. She was treated so abominably during her lifetime that to treat her so in death seems like the worst cruelty."

"How did you fall in with Lindholm?" Lazarus asked. "You two seem like chalk and cheese."

"It wasn't long after I discovered tomb KV55—Akhenaten's tomb. He approached me under the guise of a wealthy American businessman newly arrived in Egypt with a wish to pursue his passion for Egyptology. I suppose some of it was true. He seemed to have a passable layman's knowledge of Egyptology, and I have to confess that I was seduced by his wealth and the idea of a rich foreigner financing my future digs."

"Seduced?"

"Oh, not like that! Goodness! But perhaps as a fellow antiquarian, you have some understanding of the constant need to fundraise. It is a daily struggle. Money simply soaks into the sand here. No, my attraction to him was purely on a professional level. Where else would I get the proper funds needed to explore my theories that a second city to the Aten was out here somewhere?"

Lazarus felt a deep gush of relief, although he could not account for it. Before he had met Eleanor, he found the idea of Thackeray's fiancé running off with another man highly amusing. Now that he had met her he could not see the funny side at all. "So you dislike the man?"

"Intensely. We live up at the dig together and converse only when it is in our mutual interest. The rest of the time he works on his projects and I on mine. We sleep on opposite sides of the complex. But I am in a quandary. I wish I had never met him, but at the same time how would I have found the City of the Silver Aten without his help?"

"What are his intentions towards you once his work is complete? It seems terribly unfair to let you make this fantastic discovery and then shroud it in secrecy so you might not even get the recognition you deserve."

"I suppose he will relinquish the site to me once he is done using it as his private laboratory. Then I will be able to reveal my discovery to the world, and see that the artifacts there receive the proper protection and respect they deserve."

"And Lindholm?"

"He will take his monstrosities back where he came from."

"I was afraid of that. I can't let him do it, Eleanor."

"Isn't the British Empire on friendly terms with the Confederate States?"

"Yes. But you've seen those creatures. No sane person would allow them or the research behind them to fall into the hands of a foreign nation, friend or foe. The C.S.A. would build an army of such monsters and I can't stand by and let it happen. Will you help me?"

"I would dearly like to help you, Lazarus, for you seem like a fine and decent man and God knows there are few enough of those in the world. But I am tied to Lindholm..."

"You are not his prisoner," Lazarus stated firmly.

"It is good of you to say so, but I fear that I am."

"Look around you! You are in Cairo, in my company, and he is out in the desert still. What is to prevent you from taking the first steamer back to England?"

"I cannot leave the artifacts and the mummy of Kiya alone in his hands," she replied. "They mean too much to me. It is only my promise that I will return to him that stays his hand from turning her into one of those abominations."

"You would sacrifice your freedom for a three-thousand year old mummy?"

"I told you that I feel a bond with her. And... there's more. If I were to go with you, you would reunite me with Henry?"

"I suppose so."

"Lazarus, please believe me when I tell you that

there has been nothing... *sordid* between Lindholm and I."

"I do believe you, I promise."

"It's just that, well, I know I should feel lucky in marrying Henry, but..."

"You don't want to return to him," said Lazarus, allowing a faint smile of triumph to cross his face.

"Do you know that he wants me to give up archaeology once we are married?"

"He doesn't!"

"That is something I can never do. But what I *can* do right now, I have no idea. Both our families expect us to get married, how can I call the whole thing off?"

"That's not something you need to worry about now," said Lazarus, placing a gentle hand on her arm. "One megalomaniac at a time, eh?"

She allowed herself to giggle at that. "You have a history with my fiancé, don't you? Although, he's never mentioned you."

"I am as sore a memory for him as he is for me, I fear. We were once the greatest of friends."

"I find that hard to believe."

"Oh, we were never anything alike. He was so headstrong and a fine upholder of imperialism. I was somewhat less proud of my country's dominance of the seas. But we shared a common interest; the pursuit of ancient civilizations and lost cultures. We were working together at the ruined city of Great Zimbabwe, trying to establish its trade routes to the coast."

"Great Zimbabwe?" she exclaimed, her eyebrows raised in surprise. "You were part of that expedition? He never said..."

"We had a falling out. While he was suffering from

fever miles from the site, I was approached by an agent of the British government. He offered me a chance to find what he thought was the source of King Solomon's great wealth."

"Yes, Solomon's mines! Henry is convinced they and Great Zimbabwe are one and the same."

"The very cause of our falling out. You see, while Henry was at death's door, I and this British agent found a much more likely site miles away. I do not believe it really was the mines of Solomon, but the nature of our business there meant that I could not speak of it or give any indication of its location. Henry was furious and felt like I was shutting him out. He thought I had found King Solomon's mines and was keeping it to myself.

"He got back to England before me and immediately began slandering me to the Royal Archaeological Society. He also claimed that I had promised to pay for the expedition, which was an outright lie. The costs were to be divided between us. When I returned, I was forced to pay and that cost me dear. Then we got involved in a very public quarrel. He would criticize my methods in the papers and then I would discredit his theories about Great Zimbabwe being King Solomon's mines. It all got rather childish, I'm afraid."

They found a quiet cafe to have tea in and whiled away a few hours talking about other things. She quizzed him about his work for the government and he told her all he felt that he could.

"I must say, it all sounds terribly exciting," she said. "To think that a government would employ antiquarians and archaeologists as special agents."

"Anything that might help them dig up loot to

finance their expansion," said Lazarus, with accustomed cynicism.

"It's getting late," she said, looking at the lengthening shadows.

"Allow me to walk you back to your hotel," said Lazarus. "Where are you staying?"

"On my boat. A steam-powered *dahabeah*. It's really quite comfortable."

They walked together down to Port Bulaq and Lazarus saw for himself her mode of transport and residence. It was the usual size for a *dahabeah*, only without the sails. Instead, a single funnel poked up, like on a steamship.

She turned to him at the gangplank. "What would you say to taking an aperitif with me on board? We could go out for dinner, perhaps."

Lazarus was sorely tempted. "I'm not sure that would be such a good idea."

"Oh, my servants are on board," she replied. "It would be quite proper, I'm sure."

"I'm sure you know that it wouldn't be," he replied.

"Yes, I suppose you're right," she said, not masking her disappointment. "I suppose you'll be dining with that Russian woman. Are you at all...?"

"Katarina? Good Lord, no! We occasionally find our paths crossing in the pursuit of our respective government's interests, but we don't actually get on all that well at all."

"I see. Well, goodnight, Lazarus." She leaned forward to kiss him on his cheek. It was only a small mark of affection but it made him burn inside. "I'm beginning to think that I fell in with the wrong one who returned from that African expedition," she said.

CHAPTER ELEVEN

In which two warnings are given and both go unheeded

Lazarus wasn't tired, and decided to take a walk along the docks. He passed the rows of *dahabeahs* and steamers, deep in thought. His cheek burned where Eleanor had kissed him and he felt a churning in his gut—a churning he had felt before—and it never boded well. He had loved before, and that girl had ended up dead when the British sacked the Colombian village on the shores of Lake Guatavita. That event had broken his heart and shattered his loyalty to the empire he served. But eventually, inevitably, he had been drawn back to its service. The empire had turned him around and pushed him back out into the world with a gun in his hand and orders to serve Her Majesty. He had always supposed that his ability to love would return to him, but he had not thought it would come back so soon. He didn't feel ready for it.

And then there was Katarina. She was a hard woman to like and even harder to love, but their weeks travelling across America in the *Santa Bella* had stirred something in him towards her. He wouldn't quite call it love—fondness, perhaps? Despite her barbed insults, scathing sarcasm and general disgust of him, they had developed a sense of camaraderie on their adventures. And on those nights, as the clouds drifted past the portholes, the space between their bunks seemed agonizingly close, and yet it might have been the Atlantic between them. For, as much as he would have relished a more intimate or even a physical relationship with her, he never managed to muster the resolve to take any kind of step in that direction.

And so, after weeks of travelling the east coast, they had decided that they had both seen all they needed to in the United States and that their journey had run its course. They had set down in Boston. It had been raining and, without much passion, they had parted. He had doubted then that he would ever see her again and thought it probably just as well.

His thoughts were halted in their tracks when he realized that he was near the Bayoumi Shipping Company. He decided that he had walked far enough and headed back towards Azbekya.

He went to the Grand Hotel with the mind of calling in on Petrie to see how he was getting along with his studies, and found some sort of commotion in the foyer.

"Now, please, sir," a woman was saying in a firm, foreign accent that Lazarus instantly recognized, "I thank you for your help but I really must be allowed to take it from here."

"I wouldn't hear of it, madam," said another foreign voice—*Prussian?*—"until you are settled in your room and the police are called. I recommend a large brandy to settle your nerves."

"My nerves are quite in order, I assure you!"

Lazarus had to cover his smile. Katarina's new friend was insistent on playing the hero and was likely to get a black eye for his troubles if he persisted for much longer. He thought it best to intervene.

"What's going on here?" he asked, walking over to them. The Prussian was a tall man with large graying side-whiskers and a monocle. He looked at Lazarus in surprise at this intrusion, and Lazarus noticed an expression of relief cross Katarina's face.

"This man is pressing his help on me when I clearly don't need it," she said.

"Sir, do you know this lady?" the Prussian asked.

"We, ah, we're in the same line of work," Lazarus replied. "And just happened to be in Cairo at the same time."

"Work? A New Woman, eh?" said the man, his whiskers bristling. "I might have known by her stubbornness."

"What happened?"

"She was attacked down at Port Bulaq."

"Attacked!"

"I was not attacked!" Katarina exclaimed. "Do I look like I have bruises? Wounds? I was merely chased several streets,"

"Until she ran in to me who, as luck would have it, am also staying at the Grand."

"He practically dragged me back here like an errant schoolgirl," Katarina said, her eyes spitting fire at the Prussian.

"Who chased you?" asked Lazarus, knowing that it could not have been an ordinary thief, for Katarina would merely have shot them dead.

"One of you-know-who's little friends," she replied, her words mouthing the cryptic message to him.

"Here, in Cairo?" Lazarus hadn't really believed that Lindholm would risk all by sending one of his creations into the city. It was far too conspicuous. "How exactly was he dressed?"

"Like a woman," said Katarina.

"Good Lord!" exclaimed the Prussian.

"It—*he*—had on one of those long black garments some women wear here that covers all, including the face."

"That's a devilish trick," the Prussian said. "Didn't want you to recognize him, eh? Who is this fellow sending his people after you?"

"An ex-lover," said Lazarus, enjoying the expression on Katarina's face as he said this. "She jilted him and he's been on her trail since she left Moscow."

"Moscow? I thought the accent was distinctive. Well, madam, I'm sure you had your reasons for leaving him, and by the sound of it this fellow is one to be well rid of." He turned to Lazarus. "Allow me to introduce myself. I am Baron Friedrich von Eichendorf."

"A baron, no less?" said Lazarus, bowing low. "I am Lazarus Longman, and Katarina here is an acquaintance of mine. I thank you for bringing her back here safely. She may hide it well, but she no doubt required the aid of a gentleman and you stepped up magnificently." He tried not to smile at the blazing indignation on Katarina's face.

"The pleasure was all mine, I assure you," said von Eichendorf. "I do hope you will call the police on her behalf, young sir, for it would be a crime in itself to leave this cross-dressing bounder at liberty to threaten this lovely young lady further."

"Come, on," said Lazarus as the Baron moved away. "Let's get a drink and you can tell me all about it."

They took gin in the bar and Katarina related her

tale. "I had an inkling I was being followed as I left the docks," she said. "I ducked into a doorway to see if my pursuer would walk right past or loiter somewhere down the street. It did neither and came in on me in the doorway and I knew then that its mission was to kill me. It was so heavy, and was pressing me down against the door. Its furnace was so terribly hot that I could get no hold on it."

"Hmm," said Lazarus. "It seems sensible to think that this creature was the very same that murdered Petrie's friend and stole the cosmetic container he was carrying. The victim's hands were badly scorched. And his wallet was not taken."

"And so by extension," said Katarina, "the creature also stole that relief fragment from the museum?"

"I can believe it."

"So can I."

"Did you scream?" Lazarus asked her. "When it attacked you?"

She glared at him. "What would that have achieved? No, I didn't scream. I put a bullet in its chest at point blank range."

"Ah, as we know, only a bullet to the heart does it in for these things."

"I didn't exactly have the time or the range of movement to take a proper shot, so one in the gut was all I could manage to knock it back a pace and allow me time enough to free myself. It came charging down the street after me and I turned and fired off two more rounds—I don't know if either hit it—but while I had my head turned I was nearly knocked down by a carriage. I had run right out into a main street. The passenger in the carriage was that infuriating Prussian fellow who insisted on manhandling me back to the hotel. I looked around to see some sign of my pursuer, but it had vanished. Evidently, it doesn't trust the effectiveness of its disguise enough to wander into the more populated parts of the city. That probably explains why it attacked me at night."

"What exactly were you doing down at the docks, anyway?"

"Taking the night air," she replied, knocking down the rest of the gin in one and motioning the barman to refill her glass.

"Oh, come off it, Katarina!"

"What?"

"You were spying on me!"

"What on earth are you getting at?"

"I suppose it was a coincidence that I happened to be down at the docks also? It's a wonder we didn't bump into each other!"

"Longman, it may surprise you to know that I have better things to do with my evenings than keep up with your petty romances."

"Romances? For a start that's incorrect and secondly, you have just exposed yourself. How did you know what I was doing?"

"Oh, all right, for God's sake! I was spying on you! How else am I supposed to find out where this woman sleeps at night and what she gets up to on her trips to Cairo? She's my only connection to Lindholm, and if I can't return to his hidden city in the desert then I will have to go through her to get to him."

"You just be careful," Lazarus warned her. "I don't want her getting hurt."

"You're her guardian angel now, are you? Good God, man she's got you wrapped around her little finger!"

"Rubbish! She's an innocent in this whole business. It's Lindholm that's got her tied up. She doesn't even dare run away for fear of what he'll do to her." That wasn't strictly true but Lazarus didn't feel like going into Eleanor's bizarre sentimentality towards Kiya's mummy.

"Very well, Lazarus," Katarina replied. "I just think you should be careful. Or it may be you who ends up getting hurt."

"What do you mean?"

"Just be prepared for the possibility that Miss Rousseau may not be as innocent as she seems. Don't you think it strange that the mummy came after me the night she was moored up in the city? Don't you wonder where this creature is kept in the daytime? Who controls it?"

"Oh, this is going too far, Katarina! What are you suggesting? That Eleanor keeps a stock of mechanical mummies on board her *dahabeah*?"

"Well, whoever controls the mummy is interested in artifacts pertaining to Kiya. Just as your friend Rousseau is."

"Well, it still may be coincidental. Petrie only made the connection between the kohl container and the relief fragment after they were stolen. It seems unlikely that anybody else would know that the fragment depicted Kiya. Not even Eleanor Rousseau." He let the matter rest at that.

"Goodnight, Longman," said Katarina. "I'm tired and am feeling the effects of these drinks too much to argue with you further. I think I shall rest a while before dinner."

The following morning, Lazarus found a telegram waiting for him in reception. It was from London and worded in the usual cryptic mumbo-jumbo he had come to expect from Morton's office.

```
LONGMAN

PROCEED WITH PROCURING THE
PARISIAN PERFUME. FORGET THE
AMERICAN WHISKEY. HAVE IMBIBED
TOO MUCH LATELY

M
```

Lazarus cursed. Morton's timing was impeccably inconvenient, as ever. The 'Parisian Perfume' clearly meant Eleanor, so his original mission was still in effect. But somebody in Morton's outfit had evidently found out that Lindholm was no rogue scientist, but a minion of the Confederate States conducting experiments for the army. So the 'American whiskey' was not to be touched, eh? Once more Lazarus cursed the Empire's association with the C.S.A. The world could go to hell so long as Britannia kept her head above water and her friends friendly. Even if they were a lot of murdering bastards, like General Reynolds.

Later that evening he went to Port Bulaq and asked Eleanor if she wouldn't mind reopening that offer of dinner. She did not mind one bit, and they found a pleasant little restaurant not too far from the water's edge where they watched the sunset over the pyramids to the south. They seemed to glow with a dusty rose color, and set the mood for a fine dinner wonderfully.

He did not mention the attack on Katarina for he did not want to spoil the evening. He was still too angry with her accusations to think about it, much less discuss it with Eleanor. Instead they talked of other things; Egyptology, Maspero's dig at the Sphinx, Lazarus's government work and Eleanor's life in Paris before she had met Henry Thackeray.

"He can't understand why I still want to spend my time chasing down relics of the past instead of building a future with him," she said.

"Perhaps your reluctance to relinquish Kiya's mummy is in fact a reluctance to relinquish Egyptology itself," said Lazarus.

"Perhaps. But I really do feel for that woman. I want to get her remains and effects out of Egypt as soon as possible."

"Out of Egypt? There's certain difficulties with that, as you and Lindholm had no concession to dig there. Maspero would likely see you both as treasure hunters, despite your previous archaeological successes."

"I know, and yet, if I tell anybody, the site will be taken away from me and Kiya will wind up in the basement of the Bulaq Museum. I must get her to Paris. There, in the Louvre, she can receive the honor she deserves, surrounded by the artifacts I found at Akhetaten—not to mention being reunited with her husband. Will you help me do it, Lazarus? Please say that you will!"

"Eleanor, I'm not really in the business of smuggling antiquities out of Egypt. Not only do I disagree with the practice but it's not in my line of work. Please do not misunderstand, I do not put you in the same class as those who would despoil Egypt of its treasures. I know that you have the interests of knowledge and preservation at heart. But it's simply not my mission here."

She bit her lip. "What if I help you stop Lindholm. Would you help me then?"

He thought for a moment. If Maspero or the police found out that he was aiding in the removal of artifacts, it would ruin his previous reputation as an Egyptologist. But then, he was a governmental agent now and he hadn't worked on a dig in years and was unlikely to ever again. And Eleanor was no treasure hunter. She was a dedicated Egyptologist who had fallen in with the wrong man, and now her work was about to suffer for it. Could he let that happen? "Very well," he told her. "I'll help you get the items to Paris. But how will you get them to Cairo under Lindholm's nose?"

"Leave that to me. There is room on my *dahabeah*. Now tell me how I can help you."

"I need to know how Lindholm is planning to get his monsters to the C.S.A. Smuggling a mummy to Paris is one thing, but he has several and they would weigh a great deal more."

"I don't know. But I will try to find out."

"I don't want you putting yourself at risk. Do nothing that might jeopardize your relationship with Lindholm for the time being."

"Oh, don't worry about me, Lazarus. I shall be as quiet as a mouse and twice as sneaky. I'm sure I can find out something back at the site. He leaves things lying around, you know."

"When do you return?"

"Tonight. I shall come back to Cairo in a week's time. I hope I will have some information for you then. Will you make the arrangements for the transportation of my goods while I am away?"

"I shall do my best."

"Then I will have them on board when I return."

They finished eating and took a stroll down the waterfront, looking at the boats and the play of the silvery moonlight on the gently lapping waters. Lazarus grew aware that they were approaching Eleanor's *dahabeah.*

"Thank you for tonight," she said, turning to him. Her skin looked like coffee and cream in the light, smooth and perfect. "It's been wonderful to speak with a sane human being for once. And one so nice..." She let the unfinished sentence hang in the air between them. "I suppose I would be presuming too much to offer the invitation for a nightcap on my boat? It's just that you finally agreed to have dinner with me and..."

"Yes," said Lazarus quickly, before his better judgment could interfere. He was tired of being so damned proper all the time. "I'd love to."

She beamed at him and led him up the gangplank and down into the cozy cabin below. It was well fitted out. Sketches—perhaps her own—hung in frames on the dark wood paneling. A well-stocked library of books on all manner of subjects filled one wall, and a comfortable armchair and ottoman occupied the corner beneath a hurricane lamp. A walnut chaise-longue with green velvet upholstery sat opposite it. She bid him remove his coat and hat and sit down.

"The comfort of this must be a tempting alternative to sleeping in tombs," he said as she poured them both brandies from a little bar.

"But alas, it is moored too far from our site for me to use it for anything but travelling," she told him, sitting down close and swirling the dark amber liquid around in the glasses before handing one to him. He could smell her perfume and was struck by how apt Morton's codename for her was. She smelled like the most fragrant breezes of Parisian society.

"Where are your servants?" Lazarus asked her.

"Yusef is sleeping on deck and Ardath is in the city procuring supplies for me," she replied. "We will not be disturbed, I assure you."

Lazarus nearly choked on his cognac. The forwardness of this woman would give Katarina a run for her money. "That's not why I was asking! I meant, do you not feel vulnerable? A beautiful woman like you alone on a *dahabeah* overnight in the docks with only two servants to guard you?"

"I am very well protected, have no fear, Galahad. And am I beautiful? Goodness, Lazarus, are you trying to seduce me?"

He could feel the color rising up around his stiff collar and he yearned to cast if off. "Nothing of the sort!"

She laughed. "I am sorry. I was only teasing you. I am so very lonely here in Egypt with nobody to offer me stimulating conversation and sporting banter. I couldn't resist toying with you. Do you forgive me?"

"Of course. But you have Henry, back in London. Does not the thought of his love comfort you on lonely nights?"

"Now *you* are toying with *me*, Lazarus and it is most cruel."

He suddenly felt like a pig. Of course he was toying with her. Thackeray was about as affectionate as a bulldog with piles. "I'm sorry."

"You know that I don't love Henry, you must know that by now. I am a doomed woman, Lazarus. I am little more than a girl and have never loved a man and yet once I am married to Henry, love will be forever denied me. Please, Lazarus, do me one service. Kiss me."

"K... kiss you?" he managed, alarmed by how close those full, wet lips were to his own, and he was mesmerized by those dark, intoxicating eyes.

"Are you going to pretend that you are not attracted to me now?" she said in a voice that was almost a whisper, her sweet breath brushing his cheeks. "Don't make a fool of me, Lazarus. Admit that you find me lovely. Because I find you simply wonderful."

"I do find you lovely, Eleanor," he said, rolling her name around in his mouth as if it were a sweet delicacy. "So very lovely. But it would not be proper—worse, it would not be right. You are engaged to a man who is... was my..."

"Friend? No longer. Don't pretend that. But this is not about Henry. This is about us. Kiss me so that I know what it is like to be kissed by a man who knows how to show a woman some affection, a man with a heart instead of a block of ice, a man who would love me instead of use me to his own ends."

Lazarus gave in and leaned forward just an inch to allow those glorious, all-encompassing lips to latch onto his own. *This is madness!* he thought in a wild grasp at sanity that was rapidly sailing out of his reach. *But God, it feels so good!*

She leaned in close. He allowed his hand to gently touch the crinkles in the crushed silk of her dress. He moved it north and grasped her firmly around her corset, and he pulled her closer. She did not mind and they leaned back against the velvet of the chaise-longue, still kissing, gripped in an embrace that felt like it would last forever.

He started as her hand wound its way down to the lump in his breeches. It unfastened his belt and slipped inside like an asp encircling his most vulnerable spots, an asp that could strike at any moment. And he welcomed it.

Oh, God, he welcomed its venom.

CHAPTER TWELVE

In which the mummy strikes again

Lazarus spent the next few days making the arrangements to ship Eleanor's boxes out of Egypt. He booked transport for them on a steamer headed for Marseille, and recruited Petrie's help in filling out the customs forms and forging the licenses. But Petrie was no fool. He went along with the idea without asking questions, but in his room late one evening over their brandies, he confronted Lazarus on the matter.

"I know that you are an honorable man, Lazarus," he said, "And that you, like me, prize the relics of antiquity far higher than any commercial value they might present. But I must know, what is it that you are so intent on getting out of the country? If it has something to do with your work then say no more, for I'll not pry into the secret matters of Her Majesty's government. But I have the horrible feeling that all this has something to do with that Rousseau woman."

Lazarus forced a grin onto his face. He was a careful man and it was not often that he was tumbled. "You've got me, Flinders," he admitted. "It has everything to do with her. I can't lie to you, but I must ask you to keep what I am about to tell you under your hat."

Petrie sighed and peered down into his glass. "I'd like to promise you that, Lazarus, but I am a professional man and if you're involved in something that threatens the heritage of this land, I'm afraid that I will be forced to alert the proper authorities."

"I quite sympathize with you, Flinders, but I hope that I can persuade you that I have acted with Egypt's best interests in mind. Well, to my way of thinking," he faltered for a moment, "one museum is as good as another, and there are plenty of Egyptian artifacts already in the British museum, and the Louvre for that matter..."

"I think you'd best spit it out, old boy," said Petrie, his eyes narrowed at Lazarus.

"Eleanor, that is, Miss Rousseau, has asked me to whisk some items away from Dr. Lindholm before he uses them in one of his ghastly experiments. She wants them removed to the Louvre."

"I can sympathize with the first part of that idea, but why the Louvre? There is a perfectly good museum here in Cairo. Maspero could do with taking some tips on proper cataloguing of course but still, items from the City of the Silver Aten belong in the Bulaq."

"She is French, after all. And she has a peculiar familiarity with Kiya, that woman you identified on the stolen fragment."

"Does she? Well it was Rousseau who discovered her tomb, I suppose, and that of Akhenaten. It is not uncommon for one who find himself the first person to stand in somebody's funerary chamber in three thousand years to feel a certain affinity or protectiveness over the persons interred. I have not discovered any mummies myself, alas, but there it stands."

"Anyway, she wants Kiya's mummy shipped to Paris before it falls into Maspero's hands and winds up

142

in his cluttered basement."

"Hmm. And you are willing to aid in this illegal act? She had no concession to dig there, you know."

"I see no reason not to help her. You yourself said that the cataloguing system at the Bulaq Museum leaves a lot to be desired. And Eleanor has connections in Paris. She could ensure that Kiya's remains would receive the very best treatment and not be kept boxed up in some damp basement."

"I agree with all that you are saying, Lazarus, but I wonder at what you are *not* saying. We met this Rousseau woman little over a week ago and you are leaping to aid her. I have to wonder why."

Lazarus was momentarily lost for words. "Well, she's a fellow Egyptologist trying to do the best in a less than ideal situation. Why not help her?"

"And the fact that she is incredibly beautiful has nothing to do with it?"

"Honestly, Flinders, what do you take me for?"

"And that she is Henry Thackeray's fiancé is also irrelevant?"

"Why on earth would it be relevant? You know that Henry and I have not been on the best of terms in recent years. Why would I rush to help his fiancé?"

"Why indeed? I hope that you are not romantically involved with her."

Lazarus set his glass down a little too heavily. "You go too far, Flinders."

"Then I apologize. It's just that she is so very beautiful and you do seem to have met her privately on more than one occasion. After dark..."

"For God's sake, Flinders! I need to convince her to come back to England with me. that's my mission! I... oh, confound the whole ruddy matter! I can't lie to

143

you, Flinders. I *am* romantically involved with her. Worse, in *love* with her."

"Bloody hell!" said Petrie, putting down his glass. "I thought there was something fishy about the whole thing! Does she return your affections?"

"Undoubtedly."

"Well, you're a cad of course, but I expect you know that. I just hope your reasons for loving each other are true and not borne of something uglier."

"What do you mean?"

"Well, she needs your help and you need hers. And you despise her fiancé. Do you not think that might play a factor?"

"Come off it! I'm not playing with her to spite Henry!"

"I'm not saying that you are, I'm just making you aware of the possibility. I... what was that?"

His head had jerked around to look at the window. Lazarus had not seen anything. "What was what?"

"A shadow just moved past the window."

"Are you sure it wasn't the curtains moving in the breeze?"

"Quite sure. Something flitted past, like a bloody quick cloud."

They went to the window and opened it wider. Nobody in the bustle of Opera Square below appeared to have noticed anything unusual up on the face of the Grand Hotel. They cast their eyes along the rows of windows, some lit up by the occupants of their rooms and others left dark. From the sill of one of these unlit ones, a figure emerged, a long black cloak concealing its form, flapping wraith-like in the hot night air.

"There!" said Petrie, flinging out a finger.

They watched the figure move up the side of the

hotel with astonishing agility, apparently finding hand and foot holds in the bare stone.

"It's heading around the corner!" said Petrie.

"Katarina!" Lazarus exclaimed and ducked back inside, drawing his revolver.

"I'll get mine," said Petrie, heading over to his wardrobe.

They hurried out of the room and down the Brussels-carpeted corridors towards the stairwell. An alarmed couple let out a cry at the sight of their drawn revolvers.

Taking the steps three at a time, they ascended to the upper floor where Katarina's room was. Lazarus knew the number, although he had never called on her in her room, and led the way around another corner. He hammered on the door with a bunched fist. Katarina took her time in opening it, Lazarus cursing her slowness all the way. At last her face appeared and it did not look impressed by the late intrusion.

Lazarus said nothing, but elbowed both the door and Katarina aside, storming into the room and leveling his pistol at the open window.

"What on earth are you playing at now, Longman?" Katarina demanded. She was wearing her silk negligee.

"Get her out of here, Flinders," said Lazarus, not taking his eyes off the window.

"What do you mean, 'get me out of here'?" Katarina demanded.

"No time to argue. That creature has tracked you down to the hotel and is currently scaling the wall in an attempt to get in."

Katarina showed a slight loss of color in her cheeks. But before she could recover herself, Petrie was tugging at her elbow and hauling her out of the room.

145

"We had better go, my dear," he said. "Let Lazarus tackle this thing."

The shape appeared at the window like a thing from a nightmare, its iron claws clutching the wooden sill and digging deep scars into it. Its monstrous face, all rotten bandages and shriveled flesh with gaping, eyeless sockets, leered in at them.

Lazarus waited until it had hauled its torso up onto the sill so he could get a proper shot at its heart. The green gas-filled orb was obscured by its cloak and so he guessed, squeezing the trigger and sending a bullet ripping through cloth, bandage and flesh.

"Damn!" he cursed. "Missed by an inch!"

Reeling backwards, the mummy regained its clutch on the sill and squirmed forward with even more rapidity, slithering into the room like an eel. Lazarus fired again and again, trying to keep cool and focus as the monster came towards him, its joints letting out jets of steam. He backed out into the hallway and slammed the door shut.

"That'll never hold it in!" said Katarina.

"Of course not. Now help me move this couch."

They dragged the piece of hallway furniture up to the door just as it began to open under the pressure of the creature on the other side. They jammed the walnut rim of the couch under the door handle, but a further hurl of the creature forced it back.

"Christ, but he's strong!" said Petrie.

The feet of the couch were caught in the thick carpet and kept the door wedged shut. They found other items to pile up—a potted plant, a grandfather clock and a rolled up rug from the other hallway—and shoved them into position, barricading the creature in the room. Evidently possessing some degree of

146

intelligence, the creature decided that it was useless to persist hurling itself against the obstacle. The great thuds and splintering cracks of the wood subsided.

"He'll no doubt vacate the room and look for another way in," said Lazarus.

"But that could be any room in the hotel!" said Katarina.

"Then we'll just have to outwit him," said Lazarus. "And that shouldn't be too hard. Our prime concern is getting you to a safe spot."

"I'd be better able to look after myself if only you had let me fetch my pistol," Katarina snapped.

"There wasn't time," said Lazarus. "Come on, I know where I can take you."

There were cries of alarm at the gunshots, and the few brave heads that peered out of their rooms vanished quickly at the sight of two armed men escorting a scantily-clad female down the corridor. They arrived at a door and Katarina groaned with dismay.

"Please tell me we're not doing this."

Lazarus hammered on the door, which was promptly answered by the mustachioed face of Baron von Eichendorf. His bushy eyebrows lifted in surprise. "Good lord, were you involved in that shooting just now, Longman? I heard the shots and was just looking for my service revolver when..." he caught sight of Katarina in her silk negligee. "I say! Perhaps you'd better come in. All of you I mean! We can't leave this young lady standing around in the corridor in such a state. I have a gown that is yours, madam."

"Thank you," Katarina mumbled as they entered the room. The Baron draped a thick, quilted gown of brown silk over her shoulders.

"Now what the devil is it all about, hmm?" said von Eichendorf as he poured all three of them some brandy.

"Miss Mikolavna's friend has returned, I fear," said Lazarus, accepting the brandy gratefully and gulping it down. "He broke into her room through the window. We were able to get her out in time and barricade him in, but I believe he has found a way out and is stalking the corridors of the hotel looking for her."

"That bounder doesn't take no for an answer, does he?" exclaimed the Baron. He fitted his monocle into place and knocked off the rest of his drink. "There's not a moment to lose, then. Miss Mikolavna shall remain here while we scour the hotel for this character and put a stop to him once and for all. The police will be on their way no doubt, but they are much too tardy for us all to wait around while this maniac is on the loose." He slotted several eleven millimeter cartridges into his Prussian Reichsrevolver and cocked it.

"Flinders, I want you to remain here with Katarina," said Lazarus.

"But, old friend..." said Petrie in a valiant show of courage.

"The Baron and I are military men," said Lazarus, "and somebody needs to be here should the monster slip past us or get in at her through the window again."

"Monster is right," said von Eichendorf. "Fellow needs to be put out of his misery if you ask me."

"You have no idea," said Lazarus. "Take my word for it and aim for the heart. He is remarkably robust and you may not get a second chance."

They stepped out into the corridor and Petrie shot the bolt on the door behind them. The corridors were deserted. As they advanced down them, they could almost smell the fear from the occupied rooms.

"What if this fellow has gone downstairs?" von Eichendorf asked. "There's plenty of innocent people down in the ballroom and restaurant."

"He'll be up here somewhere," Lazarus assured him.

There came a scream of terror from somewhere nearby.

"Told you."

They broke into a run and rounded the corner to find a lady in an evening dress lying in a swoon in her husband's arms.

"Which way?" Lazarus asked.

The man stuck out a trembling finger towards the top floor bar.

"Plenty of innocent people in there, too," said Lazarus as they headed up the steps to the lounge bar.

The people within were sitting quietly, evidently shocked by the sounds they had been hearing throughout the hotel, and were doing their best to wash away their fear with strong spirits. Lazarus scanned the room. They were mostly Europeans, sitting in small groups, dressed in their evening attire. They went up to the bar where an Egyptian in a tarboosh was serving drinks.

"There is trouble afoot, as you are no doubt aware," Lazarus said to the barman in a quiet tone. "And it's most likely coming this way. Do you have any firearms to hand?"

The barman's eyes grew wide at this.

"Come now, man, my friend is serious," said von Eichendorf.

The Egyptian nodded and fumbled with a key in his pocket, then disappeared into a back room.

Lazarus overheard some bore at a table near the door; "Why in God's name have they started letting bloody gippie women in here? The staff are quite tolerable but do we have to put up with their wives sauntering around here in their morbid garb, or has she just wandered in off the street to beg? I'll give her bloody *baksheesh* if she comes back!"

Lazarus's eyes swiveled. The cloaked form exited the bar and swung the double doors shut behind it. "Quick!" he yelled, whacking his knuckles against von Eichendorf's barrel chest.

They slammed against the doors which didn't give an inch. There was the sound of wrenching iron in the corridor beyond. Lazarus hauled on the handles but found the doors jammed fast. People were rising from their seats behind them.

"Crafty bugger," said von Eichendorf.

"Yes," Lazarus agreed. "First we locked him in and now he has returned the favor."

"Gentlemen, if you please!" said the bartender, approaching with a twelve gram William Powell and Son double-barreled shotgun in his hand. Lazarus and von Eichendorf dived for cover as he aimed it where the two doors joined, and fired off both rounds. The wood flew away in splinters. Sparks briefly showed from where the pellets tore through whatever iron implement the creature had fastened the doors with.

Coughing through the smoke, Lazarus booted the doors open and stepped out into the corridor, sweeping left and right with his revolver. The mangled remains of a cast iron coat rack lay in two halves on either side of the door. That the long implement had been twisted by some incredibly powerful force around the door handles elicited a great deal of discussion from the men and women who were filing out into the corridor.

"Bloody superhuman!" he head one of them say.

They heard gunshots from the other side of the floor and broke into a run. "Damn!" Lazarus said. "He tricked us into the bar and now he's headed back to get at Katarina."

They headed towards von Eichendorf's room, and found the door smashed open and the room empty.

"This way!" said the Baron, heading for the stairwell where the sounds of a struggle could be heard.

There they found Petrie engaged with the creature, his face slowly turning purple as the iron claws dug into his neck. It was trying to force him backwards over the banister where fifty feet of open space yawned behind him.

Lazarus and von Eichendorf hurled themselves at the creature and tried to prize its arms away, but it was too strong. It knocked them both in opposite directions; von Eichendorf against the wall of the stairwell and Lazarus over the banister. He grabbed at the brass railing and found himself dangling over the drop, his fingers clutching at the slippery metal.

The creature had released Petrie and the Egyptologist lay on the floor, barely conscious enough to register the monster's advances. Lazarus struggled to pull himself up over the railing before the creature could harm his friend more but a gunshot was fired from somewhere and the creature's glass orb exploded, releasing a spatter of the green liquid. It stumbled in its death throes and fell against the banister mere feet from where Lazarus dangled precariously.

A further two bullets struck the creature, making it topple backwards and fall, sliding over the railing and flapping past Lazarus as it plummeted to the marble floor below.

A hand extended itself to Lazarus and he grasped it, pulling himself up. He found himself looking into the face of Katarina, a smoking gun held in her other hand.

"Another one you owe me, Longman," she said as he scrambled over the railing, eager to find solid ground to stand on.

"And it won't be the last, I fear," he replied. "My thanks. But where the devil did you get to?"

They helped Petrie to his feet. "The monster got past you two, as I expected and came in on us as if the door were firewood," Katarina explained. "Petrie was unable to get a bullet through its heart but not for lack of trying, so I entangled it in a curtain and we made our escape. I went back to my room to fetch my revolver while Petrie led it on a wild goose chase around the floor."

"A chase I lost, I fear," said Petrie, loosening his collar as his face reverted to its normal color.

They looked down at the smashed remains of the mechanical mummy in the broken crater it had made in the marble floor below. One metal limb had come loose and lay a few feet away. Its furnace was dimming and its split boiler swept the floor with steaming liquid. Von Eichendorf groaned and joined them at the railing, rubbing the back of his head where it had struck the wall. He grasped the railing and blinked down at what he was seeing.

"What exactly is the line of work you and Miss Mikolavna are involved in, Mr. Longman?" he asked.

Chapter Thirteen

In which plans are made to thwart Dr. Lindholm

The police arrived, as predicted, far too late to offer any resolution to the situation other than to ask the same questions of everybody more than once. It was Captain Hassanein who headed the investigation, and he was about as happy to see Lazarus and his companions as they were to see him. His success in cracking the ring of antique dealers had given him an even greater sense of self importance, and his attitude was insufferable. Émile Brugsch may have had his name splashed all over the newspapers as the Egyptologist who had discovered the Deir el-Bahari cache, but Hassanein's assistance, although unaccredited by the press, had no doubt earned him more than his share of recognition in his own circles.

The reaction of the police to the mangled remains of the creature paralleled that of those who had seen it when it had been moving about; that of horrified, appalled shock. Hassanein demanded to know what the creature was, where it had come from and what its connection was to the three foreigners he was coming to realize spelled bad news whatever they were doing.

Lazarus had briefed Katarina and Petrie before the captain had arrived, and they had their cover story sealed tight. They each answered Hassanein's tedious questions as honestly as possible, but mentioned nothing of their visit to the City of the Silver Aten, and kept utterly silent about Eleanor Rousseau. The creature, they insisted, seemed to be of an American make, confirmed by the mechanite furnace.

After spending the night walking around in circles in the verbal sense of the term, Hassanein reluctantly admitted that he had got all that could be had from the hotel's residents. The creature, whatever it was, was a highly offensive fusion of Egypt's ancient heritage and the industrial oppressiveness of the western world. It was not worth bothering to ask where the mummy had been obtained—mummies were all too easily available to foreigners—and Lazarus smiled to think of how oblivious Hassanein was that this particular mummy came from that very same cache, the discovery of which he was currently milking.

No, the most interesting thing was the mechanite. How had that come into Egypt? Stolen from the Americans? Smuggled here by an American? Had an American put the thing together or had it been a British scientist? Or an Egyptian carried away by the influence more developed countries had exerted on Egypt in recent years? Lazarus offered no theories on this.

When Hassanein and his men finally left, Lazarus, Katarina and Petrie joined Baron von Eichendorf for brandies in his room. They felt like they needed a drink more due to the captain's grilling than to their encounter with the mummy.

"Well, I hope tonight has put paid to your ideas about Eleanor Rousseau being behind the attacks," Lazarus told Katarina.

"Why would it?" she replied.

"She's on her way back to the dig! Her boat is far from Cairo. And besides, there is no room on board it for a mechanical mummy's sleeping quarters." As soon as he had finished his sentence he realized his error.

"So you've seen the interior of her boat, have you?" Katarina snapped. "Well, I suppose that answers the question of what you've been doing with your evenings lately. Isn't she the fiancé of your friend? Funny way to treat a friend."

"How dare you!" Lazarus protested weakly, knowing that this was another argument he was not going to win.

Katarina was on her feet and heading towards the door. "And for your information, Longman," she said by way of parting, "she could have been keeping that creature somewhere else in the city. The lack of arrangements for it on her *dahabeah* doesn't prove a damn thing!"

Lazarus followed her out into the corridor. "You are so devilishly eager to place the blame at her doorstep, aren't you?" He didn't care if they woke the whole hotel arguing in the corridor like this in the small hours. This beef between them needed to be hammered out. "You'll drum up any theory that suits you!"

"No, I'm just not blind to the facts as you seem to be," she replied.

"And how exactly am I blind?"

"Because you're so in love with her that you can't see beyond the end of your own nose anymore!"

"My God, you're jealous!" said Lazarus.

Her mouth fell open. "What on Earth...?"

"Come on, Katarina! You know as well as I that there has been something brewing between us ever since Arizona. That journey in the *Santa Bella* was as agonizing for you as it was for me. I don't know why we didn't just admit our feelings for each other and made the trip a glorious romance, but we didn't and now it drives you mad to see me with another woman."

Her face trembled with rage and she spoke in a slow, cold voice. "You've got some funny ideas about yourself, Longman. *And* about women." She turned and left him standing in the corridor.

The newspapers for the rest of the week were full of the incident of the 'Steam-man at the Grand Continental'. Many wild theories were tossed around, but few were taken seriously by the public who remained as much in the dark about matters as the police.

When Eleanor's boat docked the following Tuesday, Lazarus met her for lunch in a prearranged cafe. At once it was like old lovers reuniting after a long time apart. The public setting restrained Lazarus from embracing her and kissing her on the mouth. It took every ounce of his self-control, and he had to make do with the memories of their night together on her *dahabeah* while they drank tea, ate sandwiches and made small talk.

"Is everything arranged for the transport of my goods, darling?" she asked him. "All is packed up in crates on my boat, Kiya and all."

Lazarus was suddenly alarmed by the notion of Eleanor sleeping in such close proximity to that horrible, withered old mummy, but he put his anxiety down to his recent experiences with the more animated brand of dead Egyptian. He reminded himself that Kiya was just a regular embalmed corpse and not one of Lindholm's abominations.

"All is prepared," he told her. "I have booked passage for you and your cases on a steamer headed for Marseille where a train will take to you Paris."

"Thank you! I knew I could count on you!" Her hand touched his over the small round table that held their tea and sandwiches and he briefly grasped it, conscious of eyes looking in their direction from the other tables. He had noticed before how soft and smooth her skin was, like silk. And her perfume... he didn't know what it was but every time he smelled it he wanted to gulp down great lungfuls.

"For the time being, I think you should stay at the Continental," he told her. It's too dangerous down at the docks with Lindholm's monsters running about. If he gets an inkling that you have departed the site, he might send them after you."

"Very well," she said. "I have some information for you in return."

"Oh?"

"Lindholm is making moves to abandon the site himself. He has had empty crates shipped to him. I have no doubt he is planning to pack his monstrous creations and all his equipment into them for transport."

"Any markings on the crates?"

"Yes, the name of the Bulaq Museum!"

"What?"

"I don't know what he is planning. Perhaps he is not intending to ship them to America at all."

"No, I believe that is his intention. But I can't see where the museum figures into it. They surely can't be aiding him. Maspero would never allow it. And Brugsch knew nothing of Lindholm's involvement in the robbing of the Deir el-Bahari cache. These crates must be forgeries to conceal their contents."

"But why mask them as the property of the museum? What could that achieve? Do you think he is intending to sneak them into the museum?"

"I don't know. I don't see his reasoning in this but I will find out. Now, we must turn our thoughts to another pressing matter."

"And that is?"

"What is to become of us once I have halted Lindholm in his tracks and you have fled to Paris?"

She looked down at the tablecloth for a moment, tracing the arabesque patterns with a delicate finger. "I don't know. Your work for the British government would surely keep you very busy."

"I'm not sure that I can continue working for them if I go against Lindholm."

"What do you mean?"

"I was warned off him. The government doesn't want their friendship with the Confederacy jeopardized."

"And you are disobeying your orders? Not for me, I hope. I shall be far out of his reach soon."

"No, not just for you. I have to stop him. After having fought his creatures, I cannot let him continue his research, especially back in the safety of his homeland, orders or no."

"But what will happen to you once you return to England? Dismissal? Imprisonment? Oh, Lazarus, I could not bear it!"

"Neither could I, believe me. That is why I was thinking of accompanying you to Paris."

A strange expression passed across her face at his words, as if they presented some deep problem to her.

But she quickly beamed at him. "That would be wonderful! We could marry!"

"Steady on!" said Lazarus, unable to conceal his grin at her eagerness. "You're still engaged to Henry. Christ, I will come out of all this looking like the greatest of cads, won't I? But I don't care. Not if it means that I can be with you."

"Yes, poor Henry. I will write to him. We are awful though, aren't we? Wicked and wrong."

"Listen, if we can make each other happy in this God-forsaken world, then nobody in it has the right to keep us apart."

Lazarus returned to his room and penned a letter of resignation addressed to Morton. He felt guilty at betraying the old man. It resembled desertion. But the thought of no more gallivanting around the globe on the orders of Her Majesty's government made him giddy with happiness.

He met with Petrie that night and told him of their plans. He trusted the Egyptologist more than any man in Cairo and, although he was still met with stern disapproval, he knew that Flinders would support him and not betray his confidence.

"By the way, Flinders," said Lazarus. "Do you know of any large shipments the museum is making in the near future?"

"None that I'm aware of. I'm hopelessly out of the loop since I lost out on the Deir el-Bahari cache."

Lazarus still felt bad for his friend. The newspapers had found something new to scream about since the incident at the Grand Continental, but the pain at missing out on the biggest find in living memory clearly still burned deep in Petrie's bosom. Lazarus promised himself that he would try to make amends in any way possible once this business was all taken care of. "Lindholm is using the museum's stamp to disguise his creations as antiquities for shipment."

"Makes sense, really. They are antiquities. Bits of them, anyway."

"I know I've asked a lot of you in recent days, particularly in the matter of discretion."

Petrie said nothing.

"But do you think you could try and find out how Lindholm might be able to conceal a dozen large packing cases marked with the museum's stamp? Is there some large consignment leaving the country in which they may be concealed?"

"I'll have an ask around. I still have some friends up at the museum. I'll see what I can do."

"Thank you, Flinders. For everything."

The following day Petrie caught up with Lazarus in Azbekya Gardens. They walked together and watched the crows in the trees.

"Well, I have found out something which will no doubt help your case," said the Egyptologist.

"Indeed?"

"Maspero's fuming about the whole business, but the orders have come from the Khedive himself. I'm forced to side with Maspero on this one, although I have no personal standing on the matter of the C.S.A. Of course, you may feel differently."

"What's the news, Flinders?"

"It's all to do with this visit from the Confederacy, you see. The *CSS Scorpion II* landing."

Lazarus snapped his fingers in irritation at his own

stupidity. "Of course! Why didn't I see it sooner! What better way to smuggle items to America than onboard a diplomatic vessel! No doubt the crew and captain are in on it, probably under the same orders as Lindholm. But how is he planning on getting the items on board under the eyes of the Egyptian and British authorities?"

"That's what I'm telling you, Lazarus. As a special gift to the C.S.A. and in recognition of their visit, the Khedive is giving them a collection of Egyptian antiquities; everything from mummies and jars to busts and statues! It's an outrageous waste! What appreciation will these items find in a land ravaged by war as you have described?"

But Lazarus wasn't thinking along those lines. "I don't believe the antiquities will ever leave Egypt," he said, "so you have no need to worry about them. Lindholm will no doubt switch the cases for his own and leave the gifts aside. But how is he planning to make the switch? When is the *Scorpion II* due to leave?"

"In two day's time."

"Then Lindholm's crates will be on their way. Maybe they are in Cairo already. I have to find a way to stop them from being loaded onboard."

"But you don't know where the shipment of antiquities is being held," said Petrie. "Perhaps in the museum's basement?"

"Perhaps," said Lazarus. "But such a valuable cargo will be well guarded. And I have a feeling that two guns will be better than one in this case."

"Well, your request isn't wholly outrageous," said Katarina in the doorway to her room.

"It's more of an offer than a request," said Lazarus, his face frozen. "Take it or leave it."

They had not spoken since their argument several days ago. As far as Lazarus was concerned, he would be quite happy never to speak to the Russian again. But then, he knew how good she was in a fight. In fact they complimented each other very well.

"Rubbish," she said, seeing right through him. "You wouldn't come to me unless you needed me. We haven't exactly seen eye to eye over this."

"Look, I'm offering you the chance to grab Lindholm. All I'm interested in is stopping him from reaching America."

"And I can have him? We're agreeing on that?"

"My mission was never to get Lindholm. In fact my agency has warned me not to touch him."

"And you are disobeying them? Again? Tut-tut, Longman. Whatever are they to do with you?"

"What happened in Arizona is far beyond their comprehension. As far as they are concerned, I found Cibola, but no gold. So I'm clean as a whistle. Besides, you were the one who really betrayed your country. And you're still alive. Now it's my turn."

"Very well. What's your plan?"

Chapter Fourteen

In which another voyage is undertaken

The crowds swarmed to the square in front of the Mohamed Ali Citadel. Built by Saladin as a defense against crusaders, the walled fortress rose up above the roofs of the city like a proud grandfather, the minarets of the alabaster-tiled mosque of Mohamed Ali Pasha piercing the azure sky.

The balloon of the *CSS Scorpion II* was fully inflated now. The vessel strained against its guide ropes while supplies were loaded under the watch of grey-uniformed Confederate soldiers. Complementing this group of foreign warriors was the Egyptian army, lined up in regiments on the other side of the square in their bright blue uniforms and scarlet tarbooshes.

There was a band, and pavilions had been set up in the square for the aristocracy, the Khedive and the British Agent Evelyn Baring. Soldiers kept the crowds back, preventing any from entering the square, both as a precaution against any nationalist attacks on the Khedive and to stop any interference in the careful preparations the airship's crew were undertaking for departure.

In a warehouse to the side of the square, Lazarus, Katarina and Petrie stared at the mass of crates bearing the Bulaq Museum's stamp.

"I think they're all here," said Lazarus, looking from

once case to the other. "Eleanor said that there were about a dozen. There's at least double that here. Must be both real antiquities and Lindholm's cargo. They can't be planning on taking the whole lot on board. Somebody would notice. The Khedive and anybody of importance is out there watching."

"They must be marked in some way," said Katarina, inspecting the nearest crate.

"Here!" said Lazarus. "The corner of this one is daubed with red paint. What about yours, Katarina?"

"Blue! He's marked out his own shipment!"

"But which is it? Red or blue?"

"We'll have to open one of the crates and have a look."

"Now steady on!" exclaimed Petrie. "I managed to sneak you in here through my connections in the museum. Those guards may believe that you are part of the Khedive's team in dispatching the artifacts, but their faith in my lie may be shattered should any of them come in here and catch us prying open crates."

"There's no other way, Flinders," said Lazarus. "There must be a tool about here somewhere."

"Here," said Katarina, seizing a crowbar and jamming the narrow end between a crate and its lid.

Petrie groaned as the lid was wrenched free with a squeal of nails. They peered inside. There was a coffin within, its surface lined with hieroglyphics. They lifted the lid off. Within was a mummy in very poor condition. Both arms were smashed and the right leg had been utterly severed. Its chest had been hacked open by some blade; the unmistakable sign of grave robbers looking for loot concealed within the bandages. Mutilations aside, it was a regular mummy with none of the mechanical attachments.

"Well, this crate was a blue one," said Katarina. "I suppose Lindholm's mechanicals are in the red crates."

"Not so fast," said Lazarus as he began to read the hieroglyphics on the lid of the coffin.

"Really, Longman," Katarina said. "Now is not the time for a spot of Egyptology."

Lazarus spoke through his teeth, not taking his eyes off the ancient script. "Eleanor said that Lindholm lifted many mummies from the Deir el-Bahari cache and stored them as a supply for his experiments. This could be one of them. My way of thinking is that if this coffin is not one from the museum's collection, then it must be one of Lindholm's." He turned to Petrie. "Thutmose the Second. Was this fellow already the property of the museum?"

"Certainly not," Petrie replied. "It's the first I've heard that Thutmose the Second's mummy had been discovered."

"Then the blue crates are Lindholm's," Lazarus said with certainty. "He's planning on shipping his unmodified mummies to America for further experiments."

There came the sound of voices from the doorway to the warehouse.

"Oh, wonderful!" said Petrie. "How am I going to explain our way out of this one?"

"Go and keep them busy," said Lazarus. "We'll think of something."

"For God's sake get this mess cleared up and that lid back on the crate!" said Petrie as he hurried off. "I won't be able to hold them up for long!"

"Well, what's the plan?" Katarina asked. "Paint the red crates blue and the blue ones red?"

"Do you see any paint lying around?" Lazarus said.

"Besides, it would take too much time. Listen, you won't like this, but I have an idea."

"Go on."

"Help me lift this mummy out."

Katarina sighed and stepped forward. They grasped the mummy around the torso and dragged it from its coffin. Its limbs were so frail that the detached leg came away, trailing bandages.

"Get that too," Lazarus said. "We'll need all the room we can get."

"We?" asked Katarina. "Oh, God, I'm *really* not going to like this, am I?"

They stowed the mummy behind a wall of empty packing cases and hurried back to the empty coffin. "Hop in then," Lazarus said.

"I don't believe I'm doing this," Katarina mumbled as she clambered in. She smoothed her dress around her legs to make room for Lazarus who got in after her.

"Help me with the lid," he said.

They could hear voices coming closer. One of them was Petrie's still valiantly trying to give them more time. They struggled with the lid, hauling it up and over them, sliding it into place in the slots allotted.

The voices of the arriving party filled the room. They listened in perfect darkness. It was intensely claustrophobic. Lazarus could feel Katarina's hot breath on his cheek. Her body was pressed close to his, only marginally insulated by the folds of her skirt and petticoats. Her perfume was a pleasant mask to the stale age-old scents of cedar wood and bitumen and he tried not to think of the coffin's previous occupant lying in there for centuries upon centuries.

"Why in the name of Sam Hill is one of the crates busted open?" somebody said. The voice was

American, and Lazarus detected the southern twang in its accent.

"There was some ah... confusion about the shipment," said Petrie. "It was feared that the crates had been marked wrong and it was necessary to open them and check."

"Where are your colleagues from the museum?"

"They've gone, sir. Satisfied that all was in order."

"And only the one crate was opened?"

"Certainly. It was not necessary to open all of them. Just the one to check that this was the Khedive's gift to the Confederacy. There was a danger that it had been mixed up with a different shipment destined for some other place."

There was a long pause while the Southerner considered Petrie's words. Lazarus bit his knuckles, willing him to accept the story. He could feel the muscles in Katarina's body against him, tense and hard.

"Alrighty. Get this case packed up and all the other ones marked in blue loaded aboard. We're late as it is."

There was the sound of footsteps walking away, and then came the slam of the lid being put back on the case and fresh nails hammered in around its edges. Then, they found themselves being lifted up into the air and carried away with a swaying gait.

It was a long walk until they were set down, and an even longer wait while the rest of the crates were loaded. They were left in the depths of an eerie stillness. Lazarus counted the seconds for at least a few minutes before he dared to open his mouth but, as usual, Katarina beat him to it.

"How long are you planning on keeping me in this packing crate?" Her voice was a hot, harsh whisper in his ear.

"Wait until we take off."

"Christ! Why?"

"Because I intend to commandeer this airship and I want it clear of the city first should anything happen. Enough innocent people have died already because of Lindholm."

The wait was long, hot and torturous. Outside they could hear the band strike up, first the Egyptian national anthem and then a stuttering version of 'Dixie' to the applause of the crowd. Muffled speeches were heard, and Lazarus wondered if it was the Khedive speaking or Evelyn Baring. Eventually there appeared to be signs of movement within the airship. They felt no lift off the ground or any swaying to speak of, but the airship was so huge that the feeling of momentum was not to be expected. But the sounds of the crowd seemed to melt away as if in a dream and Lazarus got the feeling that they were rising, high, high up into the air.

"Now!" he whispered to Katarina. "Get your feet up and push!"

They jammed their feet against the lid of the coffin and thrust out with all their strength. The lid pushed against the top of the crate and slowly they could feel the nails giving way. Lazarus was already sweating in the close confines of the coffin, but the strain made him break out afresh, and he heard the blood throbbing in his ears. Finally, the lid popped free in the middle and then it was only a matter of shifting the pressure to loosen the top and bottom of the lid.

They heaved the lids of the crate and coffin off and gasped as the sweet, cool air of the cargo hold filled their lungs. Katarina was the first out, ruffling her dress and checking her revolver chambers. Lazarus got to his feet within the coffin and jammed his bowler on his head before drawing his gun.

"Couldn't you have left that damned hat behind?" said Katarina. "We barely had enough space as it was."

"Just because I'm hijacking an airship," Lazarus said, "it doesn't mean that I shouldn't be dressed like a gentleman."

The cargo hold was filled with boxes and crates but there was not a soul about. Narrow, oblong windows let in light around the edges of the hold and clouds could be seen drifting past, telling them that they were indeed up in the air on a course for the C.S.A.

"Lindholm will probably be on the bridge," said Katarina.

"Not so fast," said Lazarus. "There will be a ton of soldiers between us and the bridge. Our best way of getting Lindholm out is to bring down the airship."

"Bring it down?"

"You weren't intending to fly the thing to Moscow, were you?"

A brief look crossed Katarina's face which suggested that she might have considered it.

"This isn't some Interceptor-class airship like the *Santa Bella*," he told her. "You need a crew of at least twenty to make this thing reach any destination. And I don't fancy our chances of press-ganging the whole crew into our service. No, it has to be brought down somehow and then we can spirit Lindholm away on the desert wind after I torch each and every last one of his creations."

"Engine room's that way," Katarina said, nodding behind him.

"The best way is to sabotage the helium supply if we can't get to the controls."

"That shouldn't be too hard," said Katarina. "The pipes usually run through the gondola."

They moved to the opposite side of the cargo hold and opened the door to the corridor leading to the engine room. It was one with a large wheel lock like on a navy cruiser. Lazarus peered out into the corridor. There was another door up ahead which was ajar. The corridor was lit by gas lamps. They crept up to the door and halted when they heard voices from behind it.

Peering through the gap, Lazarus could see lots of grey-uniformed men lounging around in what looked like an off-duty room. Some were playing cards while others were reading dime novels and drinking coffee from military issue tin cups.

"Some sort of guard room," Lazarus said, backing up and motioning Katarina to do the same. "No way through there."

"Isn't there another way around?"

"That's the only door leading away from the cargo hold. I think the idea is to have men between the hold and the engine room to stop plans like ours."

"Well what now? The only other way in or out of the cargo hold is through the cargo doors."

"Not necessarily," said Lazarus.

Katarina groaned as she cottoned on to what he was thinking.

They headed back to the hold and Lazarus began fiddling with the screws on one of the windows. "I'm not sure what's directly above us, but we'll just have to take the chance that most of the soldiers are on the lower decks. We can cross over and drop down into the engine room. Give me a leg up."

The window came loose, and the hold was filled with a gush of arid desert air. Using Katarina's interlocked hands as a step, Lazarus heaved himself up and out of the window. The view below nearly made him lose his breakfast. The ramshackle suburbs of Cairo looked like a toy town on the flat, arid plains that surrounded the city. The Nile slithered below like a great green serpent, its glistening scales dotted with flies that were in fact the sails and smoke of vessels traversing its length. He could even see the pyramids at Gizah, the shadow of the colossal balloon drifting across the sands towards them like a grey ghost returning to its tomb.

Collecting his wits, he reached to grab hold of the bar ladder that was within reach of the window and led from one deck to another. He hauled the rest of his body out. His feet slipped on the windowsill, and for a terrifying moment he dangled precariously above the desert, the wind whipping past and nearly taking his bowler hat off.

"Careful!" cried out Katarina.

He almost thanked her for her concern but decided not to waste time on words and began climbing. Below him, Katarina made her way out onto the ladder, her skirt billowing like a sail. The windows on the upper deck were much larger, and Lazarus peered into one as inconspicuously as possible. It would not do to meet the eyes of a crewmember enjoying the view. They appeared to be on the outside of some sort of boardroom, which was thankfully empty. A long, highly polished walnut table stretched the length of the room. A bookcase lined the far wall and there was even a chandelier dangling above the table.

Lazarus broke a pane and reached in to unlock the window. The top slid down and he scrambled in, landing on soft carpet. Katarina accepted his help as he grasped her around the corset and lifted her in. They shut the window behind them, although the wind still whistled in through the pane Lazarus had broken.

"As we're up here," Katarina said, "we may as well head for the bridge. It's closer than the engine room and most of the guards are below us."

"Agreed," said Lazarus, opening the door to the corridor that ran the length of the gondola. It was deserted and they headed fore, down the wood-paneled corridor towards the bridge.

Surprisingly, there were no guards at the doorway. They opened the door and looked in on a wide room with a panoramic view of the clouds. Several men stood with their backs to them in front of banks of controls.

"All right, you fellows!" said Lazarus in a loud voice that made them all jump. "We've got you covered, now hands up and step away from the controls!"

The faces of the captain and his officers were a picture as Lazarus and Katarina made them line up against one of the windows. They all wore uniforms of the Confederacy, except one who was dressed in a grey frock coat with no insignias. A long leather apron was attached to the front of it with brass buttons. The man was elderly, with ear-length gray hair and an unkempt beard. There was something in his eyes that unnerved Lazarus; either it was the expression of a psychopath who had no fear of a man pointing a gun at him, or of a man who was confident he was being underestimated. Lazarus wasn't sure which scenario worried him more.

"Now," said Katarina, assuming charge of the situation. "We are going to take this airship down and you lot are going to do it for us. Who's the captain?"

"That's me, ma'am," said a man wearing a cap with the insignia of an anchor in a wreath above his leather visor. "Let's just stay calm, shall we? There's no need for hysterics."

"Do as I say, and you'll have no cause to get hysterical," she snapped back. "I'm holding you personally responsible for getting this ship on the ground. If any of your officers decide to get heroic, then you're the one who will end up with a bullet in his brain."

The man in the frock coat and apron laughed at this. "No, I don't think you'll be putting any bullets in our good captain, my dear."

Katarina peered into his face. "Dr. Lindholm, I presume? We'll be having a chat later, you and I, but first I want this ship landed."

"I've not the damndest idea who you two are," said Lindholm, "but I imagine you were part of that party that recently trespassed on my dig and destroyed weeks of my work. We shall indeed have a chat later, but this airship will not deviate from its course."

Katarina was not one to be tested. "Do you think I won't shoot the captain dead because I fear we won't be able to land without him? Well I can assure you that I won't have my bluff called."

"Not at all," said Lindholm. I believe you won't shoot him because Amenhotep the First won't let you."

Katarina blinked. "Why on earth would some dead pharaoh stop me?"

Lindholm's smile broadened. "Because he's standing right behind you."

Chapter Fifteen

In which our heroes battle the un-dead at ten thousand feet

menhotep the First was indeed standing behind them. Part of him, anyway. The rest was a mass of gears and pistons, powered by a mechanite furnace. They hadn't heard him approach and Lazarus wondered how long it took to get these mechanical mummies fired up and running. It couldn't have come from the cargo hold. Lindholm must have a few of these things prowling the decks as added security.

"Weapons, if you please," Dr. Lindholm said.

They looked down at what passed for hands on the mechanized mummy. One was a sickle-shaped blade and the other ended in a six-cylinder Jericho gun. Presumably both were detachable.

"Amenhotep's dexterity is a little clumsy when it comes to anything other than killing so you can hand them to me directly," Dr. Lindholm added.

They passed over their guns, each looking as sheepish as the other felt. "I don't get it, Lindholm," Lazarus said. "Why mummies? Why spend all this effort on Egypt? I've seen mechanicals in the Confederate States. They don't look all that different to this. Better even." He cast a grimace of distaste at the wrinkled, withered face of the mummy, lolling on its reinforced skeleton.

Lindholm's look was chilling. "Who are you? You sound like a limey. What were you doing in my homeland?"

"I work for the British government."

"A spy. That explains your meddling in my affairs here. And in answer to your question, yes, we do have our mechanicals, fine examples of my own work, some of them. But there is one crucial element which is not apparent at face value. The mechanics are flawless. The fault lies in the organic pilots. In short, they are mortal."

"I got that," said Lazarus. "And I can see that you've reanimated these mummies using some kind of galvanic battery. But what is to stop them from being killed like any other organic?"

"Galvanic battery!" hooted Lindholm. "Nothing so primitive, sir! Mummies present a scientific anomaly. They possess a property understood by the ancient Egyptians in the form of spiritualism, and one that today's science can barely scratch the surface of."

"The ancient Egyptians never intended their mummified remains to be reanimated," said Lazarus. "They saw them merely as corporeal houses for the soul."

"I see I am dealing with an educated man, spy though you may be," said Lindholm. "Then perhaps you are aware of the ancient Egyptian concepts of '*Ka*' and '*Ba*'."

"Yes, the *Ka* is the vital spark, or life as it were. Much like the soul in Judeo-Christian theology, it lives on after death but is confined to the tomb, inhabiting the mummy or effigies of the deceased. The *Ba* is the personality and is the part of the soul that is judged by the gods. Only when judgment is passed, can *Ka* and *Ba* be reunited and the complete soul make its transition to the afterlife. The delay caused by this judgment is the reason for mummification; the postponing of decay to prolong the *Ba*'s chances of returning to reunite with the *Ka*.

"Quite correct, if a little too spiritual for my tastes," said Lindholm. "Through my studies I have discovered that both *Ka* and *Ba* do in fact exist."

Lazarus raised his eyebrow skeptically. "You have ascertained the existence of the soul?" It was unthinkable. Millennia of theological debate suddenly resolved by this Confederate scientist. *And yet, he has brought the dead back to life.*

"Soul?" Lindholm pondered, tugging on his side whiskers with a gloved hand. "Not as such. You see, there is a science behind all this, I do assure you. And the word 'soul' is a gross simplification, I'm afraid. The *Ka* and the *Ba* are more like energy sources, and like all energy sources they have only to be tapped to be mastered. Energy does not deteriorate over time, as I'm sure you know. Change form, yes, but the ancient Egyptians perfected the art of preventing that change. Those old priests left me their legacy in their own simple way and now I, the scientist—which is the priest of the modern age, you understand—have picked up the gauntlet."

"You do realize that we will do all that we can to ensure this airship never reaches American shores," Lazarus told him.

Lindholm smiled. "You are in no position to make threats, sir." A thought suddenly seemed to occur to him, and a brief expression of uncertainty crossed his face. "How many of you are there? Just the two of you?"

Lazarus and Katarina smiled and said nothing, both enjoying this little triumph over the maniac's ego.

Lindholm turned to his mummy. "Search the ship! Look everywhere. If you find any more stowaways, kill them!"

The monster shambled off down the corridor. Before Lindholm had a chance to turn back to his captives, Katarina slammed the heel of her boot against the iron door, swinging it shut. Lazarus barreled into Lindholm, knocking him sprawling before any of the officers could draw their weapons. Katarina spun the wheel lock just in time before the hulk of the creature, realizing it had been locked out, returned and slammed itself against the bridge door.

Side arms were drawn and leveled at Lazarus, who battled with Lindholm for control of his pistol. Nobody pulled any triggers for fear of hitting the esteemed scientist. Lazarus had his hand around the barrel of the Enfield, and Lindholm held the butt. His finger stretched around the trigger. A shot went off, missing Lazarus's scalp by inches, instead hitting the bulkhead with a loud 'doinggg!' sound.

"Don't hit any of the windows, for God's sake!" cried out the captain.

Lazarus shifted his grip and swung the gun around over Lindholm's right shoulder. Two more shots went off accidentally before Lindholm gathered his wits and sunk his teeth into Lazarus's arm at the elbow. Lazarus cried out and drove his knee into the doctor's thigh, nearly breaking the bone. The man went down with a scream of agony, and Lazarus finished him with a downwards slam of his elbow to the forehead.

Then, the crew opened fire. Lazarus immediately

dropped as several bullets whistled overhead and ricocheted off the iron door which was still under attack by the creature on the other side. Lazarus grabbed his gun from where it had fallen to the deck and fired twice, killing a lieutenant.

Katarina had also seized her own pistol and began firing like a demon. Two more fell and slumped over their control desks. Lazarus saw that the captain was already dead. He couldn't remember how that had happened but surmised that he must have caught one or both of the shots Lindholm had got off in the struggle. With the captain and three of his crew dead, landing the airship suddenly presented more of a challenge.

"No, don't!" he yelled as Katarina felled yet another officer. "We need some of them alive!"

"Are you frightened of landing this thing on your own?" she said. "You did pretty well landing the *Santa Bella,* as I recall."

"Do you really think this is the same thing? You don't just toss a mooring rope around a church spire."

"Have it your way. Look, there's one left. Will he do?"

She indicated a youngish man cowering behind a desk and gibbering for mercy. There was a sizable wet patch seeping through the front of his grey breeches. He tossed his revolver towards them in surrender.

The incessant slams of the mummy against the door to the bridge showed no signs of relenting. "He'll be through that in no time," Lazarus said, eyeing the bending hinges and bulging of the iron. We might not have time to land before he's upon us."

"Then we'll just have to convince the good doctor to dispatch new orders."

179

"Can't. He's out cold."

Katarina glanced at the unfamiliar controls all around her. "Then we're in trouble."

The door was bending further out of shape with every crashing jolt from the other side. Lindholm was passed out at their feet and the gibbering officer was in no fit state to help them.

"You know what this means," Lazarus said.

"What?"

"Revert to plan A."

"Oh, God."

Lazarus aimed his pistol at a window and shot out the glass. Wind whipped in, sending razor shards all around the bridge. Lazarus poked his head out and looked along the length of the gondola. There was a horizontal ladder running along the roof, accessible via a series of iron rungs that passed by the window, close enough to reach.

He grabbed hold of one rung and swung himself out onto the ladder, not making the mistake of looking down this time. Katarina followed him and they made their way as quickly and as carefully as possible to the top of the gondola, shaded by the massive bulk of the balloon.

"We could sever the helium pipe that leads into the balloon," Katarina suggested.

"That's the ticket," Lazarus replied. "It'll be up at the other end, leading from the aft."

They walked carefully along the top of the gondola, stepping between the iron rungs that promised a good handhold should either of them slip.

"Lazarus!" Katarina cried as a shape made its way up onto the walkway behind them. The mummy had finally broken through the door to the bridge and had followed them up.

"Walk quicker," were Lazarus's only words of advice. He didn't fancy tangling with that thing up on the precarious walkway.

They could hear its metal feet stumbling and tripping over the rungs as it tried to catch up with them. It was too much to hope for, Lazarus supposed, that it might trip and slide off the gondola to perish hundreds of feet below. Would a fall like that even kill one of these things? Surely it would rupture the glass orb concealing its heart. They would have to hope so.

"Damn, how many of these things are up and running?" Katarina yelled, flinging out a finger at a second mechanical mummy scrambling up ahead of them. It was the one with the mechanized hindquarters of a jackal that they had encountered in the City of the Silver Aten.

"Now we're for it!" said Lazarus, for they were trapped between the two advancing mummies and the gap was growing smaller with every juddering footstep.

"We'll have to fight them here!" Katarina said, drawing her pistol and firing off a shot at their pursuer. "You keep that dog-man whatever it is off us!"

"It's too far off for me to get a clear shot," Lazarus replied, drawing his gun on Katarina's target and squeezing off a round.

They both fired until their chambers were empty. They reloaded and started to fire some more. Bullets tore through decayed flesh, eliciting puffs of dust and powdered bandage which were instantly whipped away on the wind.

"Come on... come on..." urged Lazarus through gritted teeth. Surely one of them would get a lucky hit and pierce the heart. But all the while the jackal-man was loping closer and closer.

"Got it!" Katarina yelled.

Lazarus nearly whooped in the American fashion but remembered himself just in time. The modified form of Amenhotep the First stumbled backwards, green liquid spurting out of his ruptured orb. He fell back and hit the deck, rolled, and then slid down, his metal limbs scraping against the hull of the gondola and leaving deep scores as he vanished into the view below.

Lazarus was about to turn to assess the progress of their secondary threat but realized how they had underestimated the speed of the steam-powered jackal legs. The iron claw grasped his shoulder and wrenched him hard to the left, tearing his flesh.

In a panic, he caught the arm that had grasped him and held on for dear life as the soles of his feet slipped on the sleek metal deck. The creature tried to shake him free and, finding that his prey was reluctant to let go, took a step forwards.

"N... no! D... don't!" Lazarus managed as the iron claws of the creature's right foot slipped on the metal. Lazarus gargled a scream as the creature skidded and toppled forwards and they both began their descent to the distant desert below.

Something painfully hard caught Lazarus in the ribs and knocked the breath from him. He had given up his grip on the creature as soon as he realized that it too was going to take the plunge with him, but now they were both tangled against the stud on the side of the gondola that fastened the guy lines of the balloon to the vessel. Squirming to get free, Lazarus aimed his pistol at the stud and, gripping one line tightly, fired, blasting some of the lines free.

Instantly he was swept away by gravity, like the weight on a pendulum, and carried along the length of the gondola. *Well, that's one way to reach the aft in a hurry*, he thought as the windows of the gondola rushed past at a dizzying speed. But that creature had kept his hold on one of the lines as well and was dangling like a dog on the end of a piece of rope not far from Katarina's position.

Had he the time, Lazarus would have undoubtedly thought of some better plan of action than the one he undertook. He was nearing the end of his terrifying swing and thought he might be able to grab hold of the ladder that led up to the top of the gondola, but then, what of Katarina? The creature would be making its own way topside and she would be standing all alone against it.

All these thoughts passed through his mind in the time it took for him to reach the point where momentum gave way to gravity. He had made up his mind not to let go.

The dangling dog-on-a-rope grew larger as he hurtled towards it. He fired twice, missing wildly but drawing its attention. It twisted to face him. He stuck his feet out and rammed into it. It was like hitting an iron girder. His legs split and the torso of the thing hit him in the most painful area possible. He gasped in agony but wrapped his legs around his foe, determined not to let go.

Possibly confused by this tactic, the mummy tried to wriggle free, using its torso. Its claws were still tangled in the guy rope. Lazarus looked down. The green orb was inches from him. He had the target steady now. He pressed the muzzle of his pistol against it. The contact made an audible 'clink' of metal touching glass. He squeezed the trigger.

The bullet tore through the creature's body. It hurled its head back in a spasmodic death throe. Lazarus knew enough not to hold on and released his leg grip. The monster, still tangled in the ropes, relaxed and hung slack, twisting in the wind.

Katarina held out her hand to Lazarus as he scrambled up to the top of the gondola. He grasped it and she hauled him towards her. "That was unbelievable," she said.

"Well, I couldn't very well leave you to take it on alone," he said.

"Your patronizing never ceases to infuriate me, but still. That was unbelievable." Her eyes were wide as if she was suddenly seeing him in an entirely new light.

"Come on, let's bring this bird down. I've seen all the clouds I want to today."

Unhindered, they hurried aft and found the point where the pipe led up into the balloon. It was made from Indian rubber and was very flexible. Lazarus drew the new Bowie knife he had purchased in Cairo and began to saw through it. Helium began to escape with a hissing sound. He continued cutting until the pipe was completely severed and trailed in the wind.

"We'd better get down below," he told Katarina. "It's going to be a bumpy landing."

Chapter Sixteen

In which solid ground is reached a little quicker than desired

They scrambled down the iron ladder once more and Lazarus shot out a window in the aft that led into the engine room. They clambered onto an iron catwalk that led around a cavernous room filled with pumps, banks of dials and gauges and four gigantic steam turbines fed by sixteen forced circulation boilers. Several wide-eyed engineers looked up at the intruders as if they had just swung in from the moon.

"Everybody stay put!" Lazarus commanded, his gun sweeping the room. "This airship is going down and there's nothing any of you can do about it. I suggest you all make yourselves comfortable. It might get a little rough."

"Get that door bolted!" said Katarina, indicating the wheel-lock door that led to the rest of the ship.

One of the engineers moved to close it and ducked through it suddenly, slamming it behind him.

"Stop!" Katarina cried futilely and fired a round that struck the bulkhead above the door frame.

"Well, that will bring the contingent of soldiers to us even if our escaped engineer doesn't," said Lazarus, descending the metal stairs to ground level. "Keep them covered." He went to bolt the door himself.

They rounded up the rest of the engineers and herded them between one of the turbines and the wall of the engine room. It wasn't long before the hammering on the door started.

"We've got you cornered!" shouted a Southern voice. "There's no way out of the engine room but dead if you don't throw down your weapons and surrender."

"We only have to wait it out," said Katarina. "How long until the balloon starts to deflate?"

"That's not the issue," said Lazarus. Once we've landed, we will still have the same problem. Us in here and them out there. And that's if they don't cut through the door to get to us first."

"Fair point. There's too many of them out there for us to fight. But I have an idea." She raised her voice, shouting through the metal to the soldiers beyond. "You fellows, we're going to come out, but will send out all our hostages save one, first! Get ready to receive them. We're going to open the door but no treachery or we'll open fire and kill them all!"

"All right, Missy," said the voice on the other side. "There'll be no treachery on our side."

"Pass me that canister of helium," Katarina whispered to Lazarus, indicating a rack where several yellow oval-shaped canisters were held.

"What's your plan?" he asked, prizing one loose and passing it to her.

"You open the door and I'll hurl this through and fire at it. It will rupture and knock them clean off their feet, maybe even kill a couple. Then we make our run for it, shooting our way free. I want to get back up to the bridge and keep Lindholm under supervision until we land."

It wasn't a bad plan. Although helium was not flammable, a pressurized canister would certainly go off with a pop loud enough give those Confederates a scare. And that might be just what was needed to get out alive.

"Ready?" Katarina said, swinging the canister back and forth in preparation.

"Ready," Lazarus confirmed and spun the wheel lock. He could hear the shuffle of boots as the soldiers in the corridor beyond took two steps back. He hurled the door open and Katarina tossed the canister like a bowling ball at the human pins before her. As it cartwheeled past him, Lazarus suddenly had a horrible thought. There had been no markings on the canister that he had seen. They had assumed that it was helium because they were in a helium balloon.

Katarina fired twice in quick succession, aiming for the canister which had yet to strike the floor.

"Katarina, wait!" Lazarus yelled. "Are you sure..."

Her second bullet hit the canister before he could finish his sentence and there was an almighty explosion that confirmed his fears. He swung the door closed again and grasped the wheel just as the force of the blast hit it. The thick metal door protected him from the flames, but the force of the explosion hurled it open and sent him nearly the length of the engine room.

The corridor was bathed in flame. The wall of the gondola had been ruptured by the blast and the flames were being sucked out into the sky. The force of the explosion had jarred something loose from the balloon, for now the floor began to tilt alarmingly under their feet. People and canisters and equipment began to slide to one end of the room. *Were they falling?*

"I owe you an apology, Lazarus," said Katarina, clinging to his arm as he hung from a control bench with the other for dear life. "That wasn't a helium canister. It was..."

"Oxygen. I know," Lazarus replied through gritted teeth. Well, the plan had been successful in that it had most certainly taken care of the soldiers in the corridor. But the word 'overkill' did come to mind.

The strength in his arm gave out and he let go. They slid together, down the length of the room, and landed in a heap of squirming engineers. The metal floor was un-scalable and they were forced to make themselves comfortable in the writhing mass of limbs that had broken their fall, groans of discomfort all around them.

The whirling shadows of the clouds from the windows high above them told Lazarus that they were spinning wildly out of control. He wondered how fast they were descending. Katarina seemed to be thinking the same thing.

"The balloon must surely be running out of helium by now," she said. "At least the explosion only broke a few of the guy lines. The remaining ones should ensure that the deflating balloon drops us fairly comfortably on a sand dune."

As if she had jinxed the situation, there was a loud 'twanging' sound and the gondola suddenly dropped into free fall.

"Again, I apologize," Katarina yelled over the wailing of the terrified engineers.

They must have been descending at a steady pace before the final guy lines snapped, for they hit the ground mere seconds later. It was anything but a soft landing. Lazarus, Katarina and the engineers were jumbled up and hurled down as if a god with a tennis racket had tossed them up into the air and performed a perfect smash to the applause of the crowd. A terrible grinding and tearing of metal filled the hull and would have made Lazarus cover his ears had his hands not been busy trying to keep somebody's armpit out of his face.

Whatever the gondola had struck—a sand dune, a pyramid, who knew?—had held it fast for a moment and now it released its grip, letting the vast vessel sink slowly, but unstoppably backwards. They all cried out once more at the terrifying feeling of falling without knowing what was below them or how far away it was. But the ever-shifting sands of the desert did not fail in their almost animated properties. The gondola settled as if a giant cushion had been wedged beneath it. They held their breaths as the sand held fast and the gondola ceased to move altogether.

The engineers let out a whoop of joy at being spared death, but Lazarus and Katarina wasted no breath on such luxury. They were finally back on the ground and many yards of corridors and soldiers stood between them and Dr. Lindholm.

They began their ascent through the forty-five degree-tilted engine room to where the door hung limply open above them. Clutching control banks and scrambling over fallen detritus, they finally made it. Lazarus helped Katarina up through the doorway into the corridor beyond, satisfied that the company of soldiers that had occupied it not long ago were now scattered across the desert.

"Uh, Lazarus," said Katarina as she poked her head into the corridor.

"What is it?" he asked, grasping the doorframe and hauling himself up to join her.

"Where's the rest of the gondola?"

A few yards of the corridor remained, blackened and scorched by the exploded oxygen canister. Beyond that lay blue sky above them, framed by a jagged edge of wood paneling and metal.

"The gondola must have snapped entirely in half!" Lazarus exclaimed.

"Rent open by the explosion?"

"Can't have. That canister wasn't enough to rip open the whole ship. The gondola must have snapped in half when we struck the sand. I've heard of sinking battleships breaking in half when the sunken end starts to lift the other up into the air."

They climbed further and peered out of what was left of the aft of the gondola. All around them was desert, painfully bright in the glare of the burning sun. Below them, at not too much of a distance lay the rest of the gondola, flat on the sand, its fore draped by the deflated balloon which lay spread over many hundreds of square feet. The sand between the two halves was strewn with wreckage and bodies tossed free from the gaping aperture where the vessel had snapped in two like a bundle of dry twigs.

They clambered down to the burning sand and picked their way through the detritus towards the other half of the gondola. They clambered into its broken end. The smoke-blackened corridor was horizontally level but pitched to one side as the vessel had rolled, making the long walk down its length a disorientating experience. What was stranger was the lack of light. The gas lamps were dead. The canopy of the balloon covered most of the shattered windows that could be glimpsed through the cabin doors which hung slack on their hinges.

They made their way to the bridge, stumbling and feeling their way through the darkness, tripping over the occasional body. They drew their pistols just in case some Confederate—or worse—was lurking in one of the map rooms or cabins to the side.

They found the bridge more or less as they had left it, with the bodies of the men they had shot tossed in new positions by the crash. The wind kept lifting the balloon up, bathing the bridge in occasional swathes of light, showing the gruesome scene in clearer detail. There was no sign of Lindholm.

Every single windowpane had been smashed. Lazarus walked over to the bank of shattered glass and peered down past the nose of the gondola at the wreckage that had been tossed out onto the sand below. By the light occasionally let in by the lifting of the canopy, he saw the mangled remains of Dr. Rutherford Lindholm.

There was no doubt that he was dead. Aside from being hurled through the windows to land many feet below, his body was so lacerated by shards of glass that he couldn't possibly be alive.

"I'm sorry, Katarina," Lazarus said as they gazed down on the man's remains. "It looks like you'll be returning to Moscow with bad news once again."

"I'd be more worried about what I was going to tell the British government if I were in your shoes, Longman," she replied. "Look at this mess."

Lazarus had to agree. His future didn't look bright if he returned to England. Perhaps they would believe that he had been killed in the crash? Yes, it wouldn't be too hard to fake his own death. The wreckage all about was fine proof. But the details could wait until he had returned to Cairo. *And to Eleanor.*

They didn't bother to look for anybody who might be alive. It might have felt callous but for the realization that anybody or anything left on this airship would likely try to kill them.

They picked through storerooms and put together a collection of items that would ensure their survival on the long walk back to Cairo; water canteens, food, medical supplies, a compass, guns and ammunition. Lazarus tore loose some strips of the balloon to use as a cover during the hottest parts of the day, when they would dig a hollow in the sand and try to sleep like Bedouins.

Katarina fashioned some headdresses out of canvas which they tied on with electrical wire. Then, looking like a pair of futuristic Arabs, they set off east, where the tips of the pyramids, older than any country, would be the first sign that they were nearing civilization.

The news of the *CSS Scorpion II*'s crash reached Cairo well before they did. The police, the British authorities and the army were so busy mounting expeditions and enquiries, and the public so mesmerized by this new astounding event in the newspapers, that the emergence from the desert of two Europeans—a man and a woman—filthy, bizarrely garbed and heavily armed, was barely noticed.

They dispersed to their respective hotels and washed, ate ravenously and, in Lazarus's case, knocked down several glasses of gin. He packed his things, placed his letter of resignation on top of his clothes in his portmanteau, paid his bill and departed for the Grand Continental where everybody he cared about in the world was currently residing.

The man at reception blinked in surprise at him when he asked to call up to Eleanor's room. "But Miss Rousseau has already departed, *effendi*," was his reply.

"Departed? Is she out to dinner?"

"No, *effendi*. She has paid her bill and left Cairo as far as I believe."

Lazarus refused to believe it and demanded to speak to the manager who confirmed his employee's statement, telling him that it was his understanding that Eleanor Rousseau had returned to France.

Lazarus whirled away from the reception desk, his head swimming. *This couldn't be true!* He wanted to run up to her room and burst in on her so that they could both laugh at the joke. But deep down he knew she wasn't there. Deep down he knew that he had been betrayed. But what he couldn't understand was why.

Flinders was out at some appointment at the museum, so Lazarus had a drink in the bar with Katarina.

"It would be callous of me to say 'I told you so' at a time like this," she said after he told her what had happened.

"But you're going to say it anyway," he replied, knocking back another gin.

"No. Only that I'm sorry."

"For what?"

"Sorry that you couldn't see straight. That you couldn't see her for what she was."

"And what was that?"

"She used you, Lazarus. Used her sex to lure you to do her bidding. Then, once you had helped her get her antiquities out of Cairo, she cast you aside."

"There has to be more to it than that."

Katarina sighed. "Lazarus, don't start shining your lamp in corners and jumping at shadows. It's not that hard to see..."

"There are too many things left unexplained. Why did she want me to go after Lindholm, her ex-partner in crime? What is she planning to do with her fiancé, Henry Thackeray? He won't give her up, even if I do. He won't accept my failure to bring her home as an ending to the matter. That is why I must continue."

"What?"

"I'm going to Paris. I'm going to confront Eleanor and get some answers from her."

"Lazarus, for God's sake, take your lumps and let it drop! You've nothing to gain by chasing her all around the world. It's clear that she used you for her own ends. Don't waste any more time or love on her."

"Who said anything about love?" Lazarus demanded. "Your mission may be at an end, but mine is still incomplete. Would you let the matter drop if acquiring your quarry was still within your grasp?"

Katarina said nothing but drank of the rest of her gin and gave him her 'you're not fooling anybody, least of all me' look.

CHAPTER SEVENTEEN

**In which developments in Paris prove that the
adventure is not yet over**

The trains from Marseille were notoriously slow. Lazarus arrived in the appropriately named *Gare St. Lazare* in Paris amidst billowing clouds of steam much later than he had intended. By the time he had booked himself into the Hôtel de France, it was well after dark. He did not eat but immediately set out towards *Avenue de l'Opéra*, which led to the Louvre.

The Parisian skyline was grim and black against the boiling, charcoal sky. Carriages clattered by, carrying pale faces and black evening fashion to the opera, or more seedy destinations. The heaven and hell nightclubs springing up in Montmartre heralded the decadent end of days wits were coining the *Fin de siècle*—the end of the century. In a dark alley lit by a hissing gas lamp, Lazarus glimpsed a half torn-off poster promoting 'The Fantastic Madame Babineaux, Woman of a Thousand Faces!' at some establishment further downriver where the seedy gin houses and freak shows squatted on the muddy banks of the Seine.

The *Musée du Louvre* had already closed to visitors for the night, but the attendant was still in the foyer. Lazarus questioned him in the best French he could muster about Mademoiselle Rousseau and where she might be reached.

"*Monsieur*, you understand that I cannot simply give out Mademoiselle Rousseau's address to anybody who asks for it," the attendant said.

"I appreciate that," Lazarus began, "but I have come from England on very important business concerning her fiancé and I..."

"I am not bound, of course, to conceal her being in this building at present," said the Frenchman, clearly enjoying cutting him off with this revelation.

"Is she?" Lazarus demanded impatiently.

"Assuredly. She has not left the Louvre since her return from Egypt. Her newly acquired artifacts were taken up to the *Département des Antiquités Egyptiennes* several days ago. Although she occasionally sends for coffee and food, her work keeps her thoroughly occupied."

"What work?" Lazarus asked.

"Cataloguing the museum's newest acquisitions, I imagine," replied the attendant in a surprised voice. "Perhaps some restoration also, for her cases included a large quantity of scientific equipment, the manner of which I could not ascertain at a glance."

"Would you object to my going up and visiting her?" Lazarus asked, but this was far beyond the humble attendant's area of responsibility and his question was answered by a non-committal shrug.

After borrowing a lantern from the attendant, Lazarus lit it and ascended the stairs. The moonlight shone through the high windows on the second floor and cast its silvery wash on paintings, sculptures, vases and urns from every corner of the globe. Nearly every ancient civilization known to man was represented by the relics that peered out at him like ghosts; Persia,

Athens, Rome, Carthage, Sumer and Babylon. He passed paintings done by the great European artists such as Murillo, Le Sueur, Watteau and Poussin. The sculptures of Michelangelo and Bernini, among others, seemed to come to life in the silver light.

It was in the *Département des Antiquités Egyptiennes* that the shadows were the deepest. Here, shrouded in gloom as if sulking, were the relics of that great civilization torn from the burning sands by Napoleon, gathered like dead leaves by Drovetti and mustered by Mariette, dragged across the Mediterranean to the French capital for all the world to see. Gigantic stone pillars loomed like frozen deities, hulking sarcophagi glowered from the darkness and golden statues of forgotten gods and pharaohs glinted in the light from the gas lamp.

Lazarus shivered as he passed the decayed forms of the mummies that peered from behind panes of glass, their rotten bandages and browned, wrinkled bodies frighteningly animated in the dim light, stirring memories within him of just how animated these things could become.

The glow of a light was up ahead. Lazarus saw a woman's form bent over a table, examining something. It was Eleanor. As he approached, he saw that the object of her examination was a mummy. He set down his lamp. She might have heard him coming or she might have expected him. Either way she showed no surprise.

"Why did you run from me, Eleanor?" he asked her.

She sighed and set down the instrument she was holding. "Did you follow me all the way to Paris to ask me that? Are you a foolish schoolboy with a crushed heart?"

Lazarus gritted his teeth in the face of her frostiness. "So it was all an act designed to trap me. None of it was real. You used me."

"Yes, I used you," she said in irritation. "Good lord, I would have thought that you could have worked that out for yourself without coming all the way to Paris to disturb me."

"Why? Just so you could get these items out of Egypt? I don't believe that even you would go to such lengths for a museum's wish list."

"Of course not. I lied to you about most things, my feelings for you above all. But one thing I was honest about was my devotion to Kiya and her memory. I needed to bring her here to be reunited with the things she called her own in her lifetime. The things that were stolen from her, defaced, smashed and left in the sand for millennia."

"Then it was you behind the murder of Petrie's friend in Cairo. And it was you who stole the relief fragment from the Bulaq Museum."

"Yes. Not directly, of course."

"No. But you were the one who was in control of the mummies, not Dr. Lindholm."

"He allowed me to play with his toys. He didn't share my interest in restoring Kiya's name to her of course. It was all 'the Confederacy this' and 'the defeat of the Union that', but he was an easy man to control, as are all men. They'll do anything for the scent of the forbidden flower. It wasn't hard to use him as I used you."

"Used me to kill him, you mean. Yes, he's dead. You used your two lapdogs against each other."

She smiled. "You understand at last. I thought I was killing two birds with one stone in sending you after him. I thought perhaps you might kill each other, more probably that you would survive, but by which time I would be long gone."

"And yet here I am."

"Yes, here you are."

He glanced down at the table. "What's with the mummy? That's not Kiya."

"No. When I said I meant to reunite Kiya with all of her possessions I really meant *all* of them. Including her husband."

"Then that's…"

"Amenhotep the Third, known as *Akhenaten*. When I found him in tomb KV55, I saw that they had used Kiya's own coffin, stolen and defaced after her disgrace, and altered the hieroglyphics to show his name." She indicated a coffin in an open glass case in the corner of the room. It sported a strange combination of a female Nubian wig and a long beard, clearly added on afterwards. The right eye and part of the gold forehead was visible, but the rest of the metal had been hacked away, revealing the brown wood beneath.

Lazarus looked down at the shriveled mummy and the scientific apparatus scattered around it. "My God, you're trying to bring him back to life!"

"Kiya and her husband will be reunited at last; their love triumphant long after those who tried to keep them apart have rotted in their tombs!"

It was now clear to Lazarus that he was dealing with a woman far madder than Dr. Lindholm had ever been. "But for God's sake, Eleanor!" he exclaimed. "You won't bring them back, not really! They won't be like they were before, star-crossed lovers mooning all over each other! They'll be monsters! Just like the hideous creatures Dr. Lindholm made! Unable to even walk without a ton of mechanical attachments!"

Eleanor rolled her eyes at him. "You still don't understand, do you?" She was suddenly startled by a light moving in the dim recesses of the rooms from whence Lazarus had come. She quickly turned down her lamp. "Who did you bring with you?" she demanded.

"Nobody," he replied, turning to see the glow of another lamp coming towards them like the headlight on a train.

She barreled into him, knocking the lamp from his hands to smash on the floor. The room was plunged into darkness. He felt her flee from him and steadied himself, feeling suddenly alone in the blackness.

He made for the distant light, hearing voices. Three figures had made their way to the landing. One was dressed in the uniform of a Parisian police officer. The other was Katarina. His surprise at this was quickly overshadowed by his shock at recognizing the third.

"By God," he mumbled as the light of the police officer's lamp fell on his face.

"And there you are," said Henry Thackeray. "Still poking about in dark corners while others shoulder the burden?"

"What are you doing here, Henry?" Lazarus asked. "And you, Katarina? What's going on?"

"I brought these men here," said Katarina. "At first I intended to come alone. I followed you from Cairo on the next steamer and have kept a night behind you every step of the way."

"Why?"

"That's not important right now. I ran into Mr. Thackeray upon my arrival."

"I've been in Paris for some days now," Thackeray said. "I received word that my fiancé had returned, having somehow slipped out of your grasp in Cairo. It wasn't until I met Miss Mikolavna here that I learned the truth—that you and my Eleanor are romantically involved and that you had even been persuaded to abandon your duty for this illicit affair. Inspector Devaney is here to arrest you as a foreign spy. I, of course, know your real business and may be persuaded to have you deported to England where you will stand accused of deserting your post. Or I could just leave you to rot here in a Parisian cell. I haven't quite decided."

Lazarus said nothing but made eyes at Katarina that would have burned her alive had that been physically possible.

"I'm sorry, Lazarus," she said. "But I am still convinced that Rousseau played a far greater part in Dr. Lindholm's designs than she lets on."

"And her personal betrayal of me only adds to her treachery," said Thackeray. "But I will still make her mine, by force if necessary."

Lazarus ignored him. "You were right, Katarina, and it is I who am sorry. She did use me. It was her who sent that mummy after you in Cairo. She admitted that she used Lindholm's creatures to steal the fragment from the museum and to murder that Egyptologist. Her mind is unhinged. She's done it all for this Kiya woman. She's mad."

"What Kiya woman?" Thackeray asked. "What nonsense have you got into your head this time? My fiancé's only madness was in carrying on with you!"

"Shut up!" said Lazarus. "You're welcome to the bitch, but she's a mad dog, I tell you! And dangerous!

Her work here must be stopped else we'll have another Dr. Lindholm on our hands right here in Paris."

"You sir, will answer for your offences!" Thackeray bellowed, drawing a Derringer from his pocket.

Inspector Devaney, who was clearly struggling to keep up with the rapid exchange between the two old enemies, finally lost his patience and bellowed for them to halt. "I am in charge here, gentlemen! *Monsieur* Longman, I must ask you to come with me." He jangled a pair of manacles in one hand.

"Wait a minute, I beg you," said Lazarus. "There is a deranged woman on this floor who is trying to reanimate a mummy. I believe, based on my previous experiences to which Miss Mikolavna here can attest, that she will succeed if we do not stop her."

"A mummy?" the inspector asked, his eyebrows raised.

"Come off it, Lazarus!" said Henry. "You can't buy your way out of this by spouting ridiculous fantasies!"

"I'm afraid he is quite right," said Katarina. "And these are no fantasies. Your fiancé does indeed hold the power of life over death."

"What nonsense is this?" Henry demanded.

"I find this all very hard to believe," added Inspector Devaney.

"Look," said Lazarus. "When we were in Egypt we encountered an American scientist who had somehow engineered the technology to bring mummies back to life, after a fashion—they require a great deal of mechanical tinkering and fortifying—but they walk and move as you or I. Why mummies, I don't know— perhaps it has something to do with the way they were preserved by the ancient Egyptians, or maybe there is something supernatural about the whole business; I honestly don't know all the hocus pocus behind it. Anyway, Eleanor Rousseau has been in on it and is obsessed with reviving two mummies in particular; that of Kiya and her husband, Akhenaten, whom she discovered last year and has been kept in this museum. It's all a bit complicated but we must hurry to stop her. Believe me, you don't want to see these things wandering around. They're not pretty."

The French inspector harrumphed at this and rubbed his side whiskers. "I don't know what all this is about, I'm sure, but I am convinced that somebody here is a lunatic; either you or Miss Mikolavna or Miss Rousseau or perhaps all three. But I'm going to get to the bottom of it. I can't have all you English fellows causing such a hullaballoo in our capital's esteemed museum!"

He made to advance into the murky shadows but Lazarus grabbed his shoulder. "Draw your gun, I implore you," he said gravely.

The inspector harrumphed at this but did as he was told.

They all drew their pistols and advanced as one, watching the shadows for any movement. They reached Kiya's sarcophagus and the table where Eleanor had been at work. Lazarus was relieved to see that the mummy of Akhenaten was still there, immobile.

"First thing is to get some bloody light about the place," said Henry, looking away from the shriveled brown flesh with distaste.

"Absolutely right," replied Devaney. "There are a hundred gas lights in this building. Why the people who work here insist on creeping about in the dark is beyond me."

They headed off into different rooms and set to work lighting the wall lamps. Soon the entire floor was bathed in a warm glow. Lazarus met with Katarina and Henry back at the sarcophagus. "Where's Devaney?" he asked.

"Haven't seen the blighter," said Henry. "He's been about as useful as a chocolate teapot so far. Why he didn't just arrest you like I told him to, I've no idea."

"You're on his turf now, Henry," Lazarus told him. "Your orders add up to nothing here."

"Well I'd feel safer if we were all together," said Katarina. "We should never have split up in the first place." She peered into the next room and let out an uncharacteristic gasp of shock. The two men ran in to see what she had found.

Lying outstretched on the floor, his stiffening hand still reaching for the revolver that lay a few feet away, was the motionless form of Inspector Devaney. Henry stooped down to check his pulse.

"Dead," he announced.

"Look at those marks," said Katarina.

They inspected his throat and saw the unmistakable imprints of fingers and thumbs, turning a pale shade of purple.

"Lord help us, she's managed her task!" said Lazarus.

"But we saw Akhenaten on the table," said Katarina.

"Then she must have succeeded with Kiya. Else she strangled the inspector herself. There's one way to be sure."

They dashed back into the adjoining room in haste with the thought that a mummy might be lurking somewhere in the museum.

"Help me with the lid," said Lazarus, grasping the edges of Kiya's sarcophagus.

They each grasped a side and heaved. Stone grated on stone as they slid the lid off and onto the floor with a dull 'thud'. They lifted the lid off the coffin within and peered inside. There lay the mummified body of Kiya, just as Lazarus remembered it back in her tomb in Egypt. Only Henry did not seem relieved at its presence there.

"Oh, God!" he exclaimed, his hand reaching up to his mouth. "No! It can't be!"

Chapter Eighteen

In which our heroes engage in a struggle against an ancient evil

Lazarus and Katarina watched Henry with interest. They saw nothing remarkable about the mummy. On the contrary, it was always a relief to see a specimen at rest in its coffin, unaltered by modern science.

"It's Eleanor!" Henry said in a hoarse whisper.

"What?" Lazarus exclaimed. "It's a mummy! Look, man!"

"No! I would know that face anywhere. I know those cheekbones, that forehead and those lips, withered and shriveled though they are by some horrible affliction. This is my Eleanor!"

Lazarus looked at the face of the mummy. It looked nothing like the Eleanor he knew. And yet, that might be the very proof that Henry was right, for who knew Eleanor better than her fiancé? Come to think of it, Lazarus had never even seen a picture of her before he had been dispatched on his mission.

"If this is Eleanor," said Katarina, "what on earth happened to her? She looks the very image of a mummy three thousand years in its tomb. Minus the wrappings, of course. What ailment could have done such a thing?"

Yes, Lazarus realized. *There are no wrappings.*

"And the more important question is, I fear," Katarina went on, "if this is Eleanor Rousseau, then who the devil is that woman pretending to be her?"

Nobody said anything. They just stared down at the remains of Henry's fiancé in the coffin, pondering the awful possibilities.

Lazarus walked away and headed back through the room where Inspector Devaney still lay on the floor, murdered by the very creature who had taken the place of Eleanor. *But not my Eleanor.* That was a strange thought. To have loved a woman who was not at all who she claimed to be, right down to her very name, was a strange feeling. He tried not to think of their night on her boat. He didn't want to think of what they had done together, the passion they had shared. And he wanted to think even less on who—*or what*—she really was.

The room beyond was the only unlit room left on that floor. Devaney had evidently been on his way to light the lamps in that chamber when he had been attacked and strangled. And in that darkness, no doubt lurked his murderer.

His revolver gripped firmly in his clammy fist, Lazarus entered the room and peered into the gloom. Statues from Babylon and Akkad stood frozen, witnesses to a thousand wars and murders, utterly unconcerned by this new dreadfulness unfolding before their blank stone eyes. He felt around on the wall immediately to his left for a lamp but found none. He trod deeper into the darkness, squinting to make out the shape of a lampshade on the opposite wall.

A figure descended on him from the blackness, like a vision from the darkest desert night. Fingers locked about his neck in an agonizing vice. Slim, pointed nails dug in with vicious ferocity. He struggled, fighting against the pressing figure that seemed to possess an ungodly strength. It forced him backwards against a statue. The back of his head struck it hard, causing stars to flit before his eyes.

He brought his pistol up and under the arms that were grasping his neck and squeezed the trigger. The flame of the round lit up a horrid female visage of rage and hate. The deafening crack of the spent cartridge turned that face to one of agony. She screamed and then all was black once more.

He gasped for air and rubbed at his neck. He heard the pattering of small feet as his attacker scurried across the room towards the rectangle of light at the other end. He scrambled to his feet and took off after her.

Blood marked the floor from the hole his bullet had torn through her abdomen. He followed the trail of gore through one room and into the corridor that led to the stairwell. Up ahead he could see her staggering figure making not for the stairs but the large window to its side. They were only on the first floor, and Lazarus had no doubt that she would survive the jump should she make it.

"Halt!" he cried. "Or I fire again!"

She spun around to face him, and by the moonlight that shone in through the window he was shocked by the change that had stolen over her face. No longer was she the beautifully exotic young woman he had fallen in love with in Cairo. Her face had taken on a terribly gaunt and drawn look. The skin appeared dry and tight and her hair was wispy looking, not the full, lush locks of midnight he remembered. She looked old, ancient even; ironically like one of the mummies she was so obsessed with.

He noticed the steady stream of blood that pumped through the hole in her silk bodice, leaking between her bony digits and pooling on the floor.

"You are finished, Eleanor," he said, using the only name he could bring himself to apply to her. His mind refused the other possibility until some further proof presented itself.

She gave it to him.

"Surely you know who I really am, Lazarus," she said, every word an effort for her tightening lips. "You helped me bring my coffin here to Paris to rest beside that of my husband."

"Kiya…" he said. It was neither a question nor a statement. He wasn't sure why he said it. Perhaps his lips needed to speak that final confirmation.

Her eyes twinkled with the starry knowledge of the ages and the burning desire for life that had been denied her for three times a thousand years. These were the eyes of a soul that had lived before Alexander had roamed the world, before Rome was even dreamed of. They had presided over sacred ceremonies in the dark, snake-haunted temples of the desert to ancient gods that are now known only as the crumbling statues and dusty relics of a forgotten age.

"Who brought you back?" he asked her. "Lindholm?"

"Hardly," she replied. "He may have been a brilliant scientist but a scientist he was only. He did not understand the true science—what he would have called *magic*—the science that my people have known since before the pyramids were raised. It was Eleanor, that wonderful enquirer with the brilliant mind, who could see that there is no division between science and

210

the power of the gods. It was she who found my tomb as she had found the tomb of my husband.

"Lindholm provided the technology to reanimate the dead, but as you know his experiments resulted in soulless creations. They are merely animated flesh, dead on the inside. I was his first experiment, and Eleanor persuaded him to complete the transformation; to pursue the power to its full fruition. But he never wanted to really bring the dead back, not to restore them fully. He merely wanted puppets to dance on his strings. I was far more than he intended and much more than he bargained for. He wanted to dispatch me back to the Well of Souls, curse him."

"So you took Eleanor's place in order to survive," said Lazarus. "Did Lindholm know?"

"Of course. Even though I drained the life force from Eleanor to fill out my flesh and expand my dried-up old veins, I hardly looked like Eleanor. It was too late for Lindholm to do anything about it. He had seen how powerful I was and knew that I could destroy him, so he bargained with me. We worked together for a time until I was ready to make my move."

"And that was when I came along," Lazarus said. "A fool at the right moment whom you could bend to your will and dispose of Lindholm into the bargain."

"Yes, your arrival was most opportune. A willing servant. And all I had to do was let you think I loved you."

"And I went running about seeing to the smuggling of your possessions out of the country because you needed somebody to do your dirty work." A thought suddenly occurred to him. It should have struck him sooner but his entire view on how the universe functioned had been challenged in the last five minutes. His mind hadn't made accommodation for smaller revelations. "How do you speak English? Or know enough about the modern world to function at all in it? You know far too much for an ancient Egyptian priestess..."

"An unexpected side effect—or bonus, if you will—of my rejuvenation. In sucking the life force from Eleanor to refill my veins and plump out my flesh, I seem to have taken in bits of her *Ba*; memories, knowledge. I can recall her childhood on her father's estate in Villiers-sur-marne. I remember her schooling and her discovery of Wilkinson's *Manners and Customs of the Ancient Egyptians* which sparked a lifelong interest in the culture and history of my people."

"Would that she had left that volume untouched," said Lazarus, "and had never come to Egypt. I too was fascinated by your country as a child, and like Eleanor have spent a good part of my adulthood in searching for answers in dusty tombs and crumbling monuments. But I would to God that she had halted her research before it became entwined with Lindholm's evil."

"Evil?' hissed the priestess. "You people know nothing of evil! I have seen real evil. I am of a time when the world was but a plaything of the gods. I have seen pharaohs murder their children and wives, I have seen cities burn and whole families put to death upon a mere omen. This world I have awoken in is a child's playpen compared to that which I knew when temples rose to the sky and the tombs of kings were reared block by block over a lifetime. You with your miniature wonders—steam, thinking machines, flying ships and all the rest of it—toys! Mere toys! There is no glory to the Aten anymore. You are all hollow! A hollow world of hollow men and women raising hollow children who will grow up to know only 'science' and 'logic' without even touching the feet of the true wonders of the universe!"

"Then why are you still here?" Lazarus demanded. "Why not return back to your tomb, to eternal sleep and leave the lives of us 'hollow mortals' alone?"

"Because that which has been awoken will never willingly return to sleep whilst there remains a chance to right the wrongs done to them an eternity before! In that other room lies the remains of my beloved, who was stolen from me by my enemies. I was moments away from bringing him back across the gulfs of time and death to be by my side once more. Together we shall put the great lovers of history to shame."

"Not while I can help it," Lazarus said and aimed his revolver at her forehead.

Her eyes blazed defiantly as she turned and leapt forward towards the window, hurling herself through the glass. He dashed to the sill and poked his head out. On the lawn below, Kiya had landed in a heap of crushed silk and shards of glittering wreckage. She staggered to her feet and took off through the darkness. Lazarus assessed the jump. Kiya had survived and she was clearly mortal, evident by the trail of wet blood on the grass. He leapt and rolled on impact before setting off on her trail.

It was not a hard trail to follow. Her wound bled copiously and the slick stains of blood on the gravel were easily visible by the light of the hissing gas lamps. She had made her way across the courtyard towards a set of arches that faced the *Quay des Tuileries*.

Good God! thought Lazarus. *She will be loose on the streets of Paris!*

The moonlit river lapped at the quay, the reflections

of the lamps dancing like fireflies as couples walked up and down the waterfront in their evening dress. A carriage nearly ran him down as he bolted across the street. He heard terrified screams up ahead as the rapidly deteriorating priestess crashed into people, bowling them over in her bid to escape into the night.

But she was flagging. Her life was literally seeping away from her, drop by drop. Lazarus gained on her by the second, confident that she could not hold out much longer. Sure enough, she stumbled and fell ungraciously against a bench which she clutched as if it were the only stable thing left in the whole swirling universe.

By the time Lazarus caught up with her there was little left of the Egyptian priestess but a skeleton dressed in skin, feebly eying him through mournful sockets. The crushing decay of millennia had caught up with her. Lazarus decided to help her on her way. The shot from his pistol rang out on the nighted street and drew cries of alarm.

The decay seemed to hasten around the bullet hole he had put in her forehead. Second by second, before his very eyes the skin withered and fell away from her body, the flesh curled and flaked and the very bones sank to the stone and crumbled. By the time the nearest passersby had approached, there was nothing left but a silken dress and a large amount of dust which the night wind was steadily sweeping away across the Seine.

He holstered his Enfield and armored himself to answer the probing questions of the police who no doubt would arrive promptly.

"It's over, then," said Katarina appearing at his side.

He turned to her. She was alone. "Where is Henry?"

"He didn't follow. He's still weeping over the

remains of Eleanor."

Lazarus looked down at the empty dress on the ground. "Perhaps he did love her, after all. I'll be damned. And I tried to take her from him. I'm not much of a chap, am I?"

"Not that it matters much but it wasn't Eleanor you loved. It was... Kiya."

"You knew?"

She shrugged. "It wasn't too hard to piece together after we found Eleanor's corpse in that coffin. I always knew that there was something off about the woman."

"And you tried to warn me, but in vain," said Lazarus. "God, what a damnable fool I am! Every woman I love dies. What the hell is wrong with me?"

She gripped his elbow. "Stop feeling so bloody sorry for yourself, Lazarus. When are you going to realize that the only woman for you is right under your nose?"

He turned to her sharply, not sure if he had heard her correctly.

Then she kissed him.

Chapter Nineteen

In which the last days in Paris are bittersweet for our heroes

They made love back at his hotel and damned appearances. After all, Paris was a little more liberal in that regard, not that they cared two pennies for what other people thought. Had they been staying in the middle of Piccadilly Circus they wouldn't have altered their actions. They had waited too long, put off their feelings for each other too many times. Now all was released like a torrent of water bursting forth from a broken dam. And the dam was certainly broken, they both knew that, hopelessly broken and who knew how many lives might be swept away in the aftermath?

Lazarus forgot all as he lay on top of her on the bed, the light of dawn peeping in through the curtains as if spying and then blushing at what it saw. He had imagined Katarina's naked body many times since he met her, although only out of boyish curiosity. She was petite but her muscles rippled as she reached up to grasp him in a tight embrace that reminded him that he was lying with a woman who was employed to kill people. Her lethality thrilled him.

When they were finished, they lay exhausted and slept naked with no covers until after noon. They did not discuss it. There was perhaps a good deal to discuss regarding the past and the future, but an unspoken agreement lay between them; this was their time and it may be short so nothing must be allowed to spoil it.

They had a late breakfast of croissants and coffee in a little café on *Rue Sainte-Anne*. Surprisingly, there was little in the papers about the business of the night before. A small headline spoke of a break-in at the Louvre and the death of a police officer. Nothing of great value had been stolen and the police were looking for Eleanor Rousseau, who had been at the museum but had since vanished. They were also looking for an English friend of hers and the foreign couple who were seen with Inspector Devaney.

Another piece mentioned shots fired on *Quay des Tuileries* and that nobody had been apprehended. Witnesses spoke of a hideously made up woman fleeing through the streets and leaving her tattered and blood-soaked dress behind, but this was put down as some sort of prank. Or, perhaps, somebody from one of the heaven and hell clubs had taken a nightly stroll in full getup and had enjoyed alarming people. As with the business at the Grand Continental in Cairo, the public paid it moderate interest. Perhaps some snorted with cynical mirth over their morning coffee and muttered something about the *Fin de siècle* but ultimately devoted their attention to more pressing matters.

"I must send a telegram to Cairo," said Lazarus as he sipped his second cup of coffee. "I never said goodbye to Flinders and I can give him the good news about the dig at the City of the Silver Aten. With Lindholm and his creations dead and... *Kiya*..."—he stumbled over the name, not wishing to spoil their breakfast—"gone for good, the site is open for whoever gets there first. I want it to be Petrie."

"That should at least make up for his missing out on the Deir el-Bahari cache," said Katarina, resting her narrow chin on the palm of her hand.

"Yes, he'll be famous for this. His name will stand high in Egyptology forever more as the man who uncovered the cult of the silver Aten. And I can't think of anybody more deserving."

"He was a big help," Katarina agreed. "I liked him in the end. Do you think he liked me? I can be a bit hard on people."

Lazarus grinned. "It certainly takes some time to get into your good graces, I'll say that. You are a prickly one."

"Prickly?" she exclaimed in mock indignation.

"I only mean, look at all we've been through together and I'm only just in your good books."

"Yes," she smiled back. "Only just. But you're on thin ice."

After breakfast they went to the nearest PTT office to send a telegram to the Grand Continental in Cairo. Partly in jest and partly as a reminder that caution was still to be excised, Lazarus ended the note with 'Watch out for the crocodiles'. Who knew what nasty surprises Lindholm had left behind in his laboratories?

When he had finished scribbling his note on the postmaster's pad, Lazarus turned to see that Katarina had vanished from his side. He had not noticed her leave. He walked into the other room and saw her bent over a desk scribbling on an identical pad. He walked up behind her and looked over her shoulder. The markings on her pad were Morse rather than words. He was about to offer to write her message out for her in French and let the telegraph operator do his job, but then he remembered that she had a perfect command of the French language. *Why the Morse, then?* He suddenly realized that she must be sending a message in Russian, which would be impossible for the telegraph operator to translate.

She stood up and started at his close proximity, as if she had been caught out doing something she shouldn't. He did not probe and she did not offer any explanation, but handed her note to the postmaster along with the coin to pay for it. They left the PTT office.

They didn't speak as they walked down the street back to the hotel. Lazarus knew that she must have sent a message to her superiors back in Saint Petersburg. Was she resigning? He thought of his own letter of resignation he had penned in Cairo that was still in his portmanteau.

When they got back to the hotel, they made love again and whiled away the afternoon in their room, until hunger stirred them and they began to yearn for the first drink of the evening.

They had gin and tonics at the hotel bar before dining in a restaurant in the lively *Palais Royal,* where they watched other lovers nestle beneath the lime trees through the establishment's gilt and wood-paneled doors.

Lazarus still had not mentioned the mysterious telegram, and Katarina showed no signs of opening up. He decided that the only way for them to confront the matter was for him to go first. They were having desert when he decided to take the plunge.

"When I thought I was in love with Eleanor," he began and then immediately wished he had started on a different note.

"Yes?" she said, her eyes narrowing.

"Well, I mean to say, during those heated days in Cairo when my mind was not quite what it should have been, I decided on one point which I still feel strongly about. I have decided to leave the bureau."

"Leave? You mean resign?"

"Exactly. I even wrote my letter of resignation back in Cairo when I thought my future was with Eleanor. Well, what I'm trying to say is, although Eleanor is gone and my feelings for her are utterly dead, my desire to resign and begin another life still stands. Another life with you."

Katarina stared at him. She set down her ice-cream spoon. "You would leave the bureau for me?"

"Yes."

"My God, Lazarus. You do have some funny ideas."

He blinked in astonishment. "You mean to say that you don't feel the same?"

"Lazarus, I love you. I hope you know that by now. But I have my duty to my country. And to my uncle. I cannot walk away from it, like you."

"But that telegram you sent this afternoon," Lazarus protested. "You wrote it in Morse and so I assumed it was in Russian. I also assumed that it was your resignation on its way to Saint Petersburg."

"You are right in thinking it was in Russian. And it did indeed go to Petersburg. But it was not my resignation. It was a coded signal to my contact in the government that I will be returning shortly. This excursion to Paris was not part of my mission, and I have been missing in action for far too long now. I will be taking the train back in the morning."

"Back?" Lazarus exclaimed. "Then what was all this, then?" he indicated the tablecloth strewn with breadcrumbs and the empty wine glasses, as if it represented everything from the crumpled up bed sheets in their room at the hotel to the late evening walks along the Seine. "Was this all just a game to you? A bit of a holiday between cases?"

"Don't cause a scene, Lazarus," she replied. "It is so unbecoming for a man to cause a scene. Of course it hasn't been a game. My feelings for you are no lie nor jest. But look at us, Lazarus! An English spy and a Russian assassin! Our countries are practically at war, or what passes for it these days. We could never make it work."

"We could if we disappeared..."

"We cannot disappear. Not in this world. Too many people would come looking for us. From both sides. And besides, there is my duty."

"Hang your duty! Is that all you care about?"

"I'm not like you, Lazarus! Please see that! I'm not hopelessly disillusioned with my homeland. I still feel a twinge of loyalty, deep down."

Lazarus was silent. He had never considered himself to be 'hopelessly disillusioned', but now that she had said it he supposed that it did have the ring of truth about it. He wanted nothing from his homeland now, and the thought of continuing to work for Morton's office made him sick. All he wanted was Katarina and a bright future free from empires and wars and killing. But it was clear that she did not feel that way.

They went back to the hotel and lay awake in the dark, side by side, each pretending that they were asleep. Then, eventually, Katarina rolled over and placed her palm on his chest.

"Damn you, Lazarus, don't let us go out like this. I'm leaving in the morning. I can't bear to spend our last night together not speaking. Let's make it count for something."

And so they did.

Steam billowed in great clouds along the platform, making ghosts of the people walking towards the carriages and wavering silhouettes of the well-wishers. Lazarus carried Katarina's carpet bag all the way to the carriage door as if reluctant to let it go. She eventually wrestled it from his grasp and seemed coldly amused by his devotion.

"No tears now, Longman," she warned him in a mocking tone. "I don't want a scene."

"Don't make fun of me," he replied.

"Well, what now for you? Back to England?"

"I suppose so."

"And the bureau?"

"I still have my letter in my portmanteau." It was not an answer and he knew it. But he honestly didn't know what he would do. What else *could* he do? London seemed to paw at him through its own greasy smoke, as if a wretched old hen was drawing one of its wayward chicks back to the nest.

"It would have been lovely," said Katarina, leaning forward to kiss him on the lips. "Maybe in another time and another place, things might have worked out better for us."

"Yes," he replied. "Another time and another place..."

She boarded the carriage and he followed her along the platform, watching her through the glass until she found her seat and sat down.

"Chin up, Longman," she called down to him from the open window. "Whatever happens, at least we'll always have Paris, isn't that what they say?"

Lazarus wasn't sure if he had heard the expression before, but it seemed to fit. "Yes," he said to himself as the carriage rolled away from him. "I suppose we will always have Paris."

A Note from the Author

I hope you have enjoyed *Silver Tomb,* the second novel in the Lazarus Longman Chronicles. The third novel – *Onyx City* – is available for Kindle and in paperback and you can read the first chapter by turning the page!

If you enjoyed *Silver Tomb*, you could be very kind and leave a review on Amazon or your retailer of choice, or even just recommend it to somebody. Check out my blog at www.pjthorndyke.wordpress.com where I post about all things Steampunk.

I'm also active on;

Facebook (@PJThorndykeAuthor),

Instagram (pjthorndyke_author)

and Twitter (@PJThorndyke).

Sneak Peek – Onyx City

Chapter One

In which a journal of some import eludes our hero

The butler who admitted Lazarus Longman to the house on Cavendish Square had the air of one who had nothing of enjoyment left in life but the promise of retirement. He was sizing Lazarus up as if determining whether he should be sent around to the tradesman's entrance, when Lazarus spoke.

"I don't have a card. I have been in correspondence with Mr. Walters and he invited me. The name's Longman."

"Ah, yes, sir," the butler said, a ghost of a smile on his lips. "I have been told to expect you. This way please."

The house must have been a fine one once, but now the floorboards creaked under threadbare carpets and gloom hung about the place like a pall. It looked like it had never been a family home. The only pictures on the walls were mezzotints of bridges and watercolors of foreign parts. Cobwebs dangled from the lamp fittings and chandeliers. If Cornelius Walters employed a maid, Lazarus decided, she should be flung out on her ear.

They entered a library, although for all the foliage about, Lazarus wasn't sure that it didn't double as a conservatory. Skylights and windows let in large

229

amounts of light, which couldn't have been good for the books that were lined up on mahogany shelves, interspersed with pots dangling their green tendrils onto the shelves below. Occasional oddities like mammal skulls and small antiquities gave the place the air of a haphazard museum.

In a wicker chair sat an elderly man with a small pair of spectacles perched on the tip of his nose. His hair was snow white and swept across a balding pate. "Ah, Mr. Longman!" said the man. He did not rise from his chair but motioned to an identical one opposite.

Lazarus sat down and accepted the old man's hand. "Mr. Walters, it is a pleasure to finally meet you."

"Likewise, sir. And I must say that you are younger than I imagined. Tea?"

"Please."

"Bring us a pot, Peterson," Walters said to the butler, who nodded and ducked out of the room.

Lazarus loosened his collar and looked around at all the plants. "Is all this humidity good for the books?"

"Not particularly. But these books you see here are not in the least bit valuable. Junk mostly, but I can never bear to throw a book out. My library upstairs is where I keep my real treasures. The conservatory is merely where I choose to spend most of my time. The bones ache at my age, you see. I only keep books in here because there is no other place for them."

"And it is a particular volume that I am here to examine," said Lazarus.

"I know, and I must apologize for wasting your time."

"Wasting my time?"

"You see, I did possess the journal you spoke of and fully intended to sell it to you, but alas, a fellow came calling with a better offer and I let him have it. I know it wasn't particularly polite of me, but I am trying to run a business here, such as it is. My fortunes of late have dipped a little, as I am sure you can tell."

"That's quite all right. I am a little disappointed though. And a little surprised that another individual should express an interest in such an obscure curiosity."

"It's not too hard to fathom," said Cornelius. "The journal, though one of a kind, is an invaluable resource on the mountain peoples of Siam. It is a firsthand account and the mysterious fate of its author makes it doubly interesting."

"The author's fate is no mystery," said Lazarus. "Thomas Tyndall died in Siam."

"Under extremely unusual circumstances, as I'm sure you will agree."

"Nevertheless, I find it uncanny that somebody who shares my interest purchased the journal within days of our last correspondence."

"You are very disappointed, I can appreciate that. Allow me to make some way in amends. The gentleman left his calling card, and you may have it should you wish to approach him with an offer." Cornelius rifled through a stack of newspapers and letters on the side table, upon which stood a Japanese bonsai tree in a glass bell jar. He retrieved a calling card and passed it to Lazarus.

It read;

J. C. TURNBULL

Fine Boots, Shoes and Pumps

REPAIRS DONE PROMPTLY

57 Copley Street, Stepney

"A cobbler interested in an explorer's journal of Siam?" asked Lazarus in astonishment.

"A hobby, perhaps. Come to think of it, I don't remember you telling me your profession, Mr. Longman."

"I didn't."

"I suppose it would be crossing the boundaries of professionalism to enquire as to your own interest in the journal?"

"You're right," said Lazarus smartly. "It would." He rose and clutched the rim of his bowler hat. "I must leave you now, I'm afraid. I'm a very busy man."

Just then, Peterson the butler entered, bearing a tea tray.

"Sorry, I can't stop for tea. This was a professional visit after all, and there is little further to discuss. Thank you for your time and the card."

"Not at all, Mr. Longman," said Cornelius Walters. "I wish you all success in your pursuit."

Lazarus gritted his teeth as he stepped out onto the street and heard the door close shut behind him. He was being given the runaround, that much was certain. What was less certain was why.

He spotted the four-wheeler and its horses on the other side of the street. It was a Clarence, known as a 'growler', usually privately owned, although it was becoming more common in recent years to see secondhand examples put into use as Hackney carriages. Often, they showed some trace of the former owner's coat of arms on the side, but this one had a glossy, black finish without a single adornment.

Its door opened and a face was thrust out. Lazarus felt he had seen it before somewhere but could not quite place it.

"With us, Longman," the face said brusquely. Lazarus immediately knew who they were and why there were here; the unadorned carriage, the two men who knew his name and had undoubtedly been waiting for him, following him even. These were men from the bureau.

He felt his feet walking him over to the carriage without remembering giving them the instructions to do so. The last thing he wanted was to get drawn into more entanglements with the government. He felt as if he had only just been released from their clutches, after narrowly avoiding a prison sentence or a swift departure from the world at the hand of a state-employed assassin. In fact, how could he be sure that these men in their carriage weren't just that? But no, why wait two years to kill him?

Two years had passed since he had returned from Egypt in disgrace. Not only had he failed in his mission to return the French Egyptologist Eleanor Rousseau to her fiancé in England, but he had directly disobeyed orders and greatly endangered British relations with the Confederate States of America. The C.S.A.'s ignorance of his involvement in the devastating crash of its dirigible, the *CSS Scorpion II*, was the only thing that had saved Lazarus from being thrown to the wolves. All aboard had been killed but him and Katarina Mikolavna; the Russian agent whom he had fallen in with.

Or was that fallen in love with?

Two years—and he still thought about her every

day. Two years since she had left him gawking on the platform at *Gare Montparnasse* in Paris like a foolish schoolboy. He had accepted that he would never see her again. His brain knew that. But his heart still hadn't received the news.

"Where would you take me?" he asked the men in the carriage.

"To see the Gaffer," said the man who had spoken.

They both wore grey suits. One had a moustache and the other wore spectacles. They had the bored airs of those who rarely left London and spent their lives passing correspondence between others with vastly more exiting lives. Lazarus knew the type.

"I don't suppose either of you know what he wants to see me about?" Lazarus asked. "Or doesn't he tell his lackeys that much?"

Their faces soured and for a moment Lazarus thought he was going to receive a fist in his face. But these two were probably more used to pushing piles of paper around than actual people.

"Just get in, Longman," the man with the spectacles said. "No need to be bloody-minded."

Lazarus did so, and soon they were clattering along Regent Street towards Charing Cross. They headed down Whitehall and turned into an unassuming courtyard beneath a brick arch. There were some other carriages in the yard, their drivers tending to their horses. A casual passerby might have thought the place a mere coach yard. Only a trained military eye would have spotted the camouflaged pillboxes high up on the balconies of the surrounding buildings.

They entered a small tradesman's entrance and climbed a narrow, carpeted stair that led onto a landing with three doors. A portrait of Queen Victoria hung opposite a rectangular window, the light breaking her severe face into a criss-cross of bars.

One of the doors led to a long corridor that extended deep into the unknown depths of whatever building they were now in. Portraits of prime ministers going all the way back to Sir Robert Walpole peered down from the walls. A secret serviceman in a plain dark suit sat by a door with his legs crossed, reading the Times. He looked up at Longman, did not smile, and returned to his paper.

"You know where you are and what to do," said one of Lazarus's escorts.

"Aren't you going to hold my hand when we go in?" Lazarus asked him.

"You're on your own, *treasure hunter*."

The two men departed, leaving Lazarus to open the door and walk in. The secretary rose from her desk and ushered him into the office beyond with a customary knock and opening of the door. She closed it behind him.

Morton sat behind his inordinately large desk and did not rise. Lazarus needed no invitation to occupy the plain chair set before the gargantuan mahogany slab and sat down.

"Good of you to come, Longman," said Morton, rising to pour them both some cognac.

"Had I a choice?"

Morton smiled and handed him his glass. "I've missed you, old fellow."

"I'm afraid the feeling isn't mutual."

"Yes, I understand you've been keeping yourself busy. Lectures at King's College, talks at the British Museum and a book on the Akan people, that sort of thing. Not to mention further pursuits in archaeology and anthropology. Something to do with Siam now, isn't it? Going back to your roots?"

"It's perhaps time that I did."

"Well it's all very commendable. Can't pay all that well though, I'd imagine."

"I do all right."

"And your father? Is he still living in that house in Edmonton?"

"Guardian," Lazarus corrected him. "Yes he is."

"Ill, I heard."

"Pneumonia."

"Second time?"

"Third."

"You know there are some very fine doctors at Guy's Hospital."

"You know I have not the means. Are you suggesting that I work for you again? Is that why I'm here?"

"You're needed. All of our agents are. Difficult days are ahead."

"Except I'm not an agent anymore. You damn near had me thrown in prison after my last assignment."

"And with good reason. Your blatant disregard for orders nearly caused an international crisis."

"Good job everybody onboard that dirigible perished, eh?"

"The truth of the matter is that I've got far too many agents in the field right now and not enough on home turf, which is where things look set to flare up in the foreseeable future."

"What's the business?"

"You have no doubt heard of Otto von Bismarck's visit in two months time."

"The Prussian President? Or is he the Chancellor of

236

the German Empire now? I haven't kept up with the situation."

"Both in effect; they have been merged. Since his League of the Three Emperors fell apart, he has been looking for allies against Russian expansion. His visit to London in November is part of a ploy to side with us and absolutely nothing must interfere with it. Relations with Germany have been strained of late, and although Bismarck is concerned with peace above all else, his new Kaiser is an aggressive sod and will think nothing of declaring war on us regardless of what his chancellor thinks. He's already begun construction on a new navy, and even has colonial desires—which is something new for Germany. The feeling in parliament is that Bismarck must receive British support if only to hold Kaiser Wilhelm by the collar.

"We're worried that some sort of trouble during the visit might stir things up between us and the Germans. Bismarck has made himself thoroughly unpopular with leftists all around the world due to his anti-socialist policies. And we have more than our share of reds here in London. You recall that dreadful business last year?"

"The Trafalgar Square riots? Yes, I was due to give a speech at the British Museum but it had to be called off."

"The East End in particular is a tinderbox awaiting a spark. Revolutionist groups, anarchists, labor strikes. The PM is worried that some of these lunatics might try and assassinate Bismarck. We've got our fair share of Polish Jews too, another group that despise Bismarck with a passion. None of them can be allowed to get near him."

"I assume you have employed all the requisite security measures."

"Naturally. But we have something else in mind. We need to sink a man deep into the red hot spots in the East End. A sort of spy who can ferry us information on the movements of these groups and let us know if something big is coming down the pipeline."

Lazarus studied his former employer intently. "You can't seriously be suggesting that I might be this man."

"It's perhaps not as exciting as your previous assignments but it's a damn sight less dangerous. Its intelligence gathering. A small job to bring you back into the fold. My trust in you hasn't been completely swept away, Longman, although there are some in my circles who believe you should have been shot as a traitor. I want to prove them wrong. You're a damn good agent and I don't want to lose you. You just need a bit of a chance to prove to us that you're still our man."

"For God's sake, Morton!" Lazarus exclaimed. "I'm an antiquarian! A treasure hunter as your man outside was so quick to call me. I'm not a spy or an undercover policeman. Why on earth do you want me for this thing?"

"For the reasons I have just outlined. And because all my other agents are tied up with more important matters."

"Oh, thank you very much."

"Come off it, I didn't mean it like that. I want you back on my go-to list and you need to show us that you've still got what it takes. Besides, don't you speak Hebrew?"

"I can read Hebrew should the occasion call."

"Can't you apply yourself and see if you can't get an ear for it? It would be of enormous help in infiltrating the Jewish radical clubs."

"Jews in London generally speak Yiddish. Quite different."

"Well, I understand Hebrew is still used in some of their pamphlets and propaganda. Anyway, you wouldn't be working alone. I've arranged for a man to accompany you on your journey into the underworld. Sort of a bodyguard. You'd be the one in charge, there's no mistake about that. I'd like to introduce you tomorrow morning."

"Morton, I still don't think I'm the man. And I'm very busy at the moment."

"Giving lectures and chasing down obscure books? This is national security, man! And this isn't just some plebs beating the war drum. We've reason to believe that the socialists are becoming extremely organized. The Russians may be involved."

Lazarus's heart skipped a beat. For all he knew about Russia, its mention only stirred up one thought in his mind these days. *Katarina.*

"The revolutionist movement is even bigger in Moscow and Saint Petersburg," Morton went on. "And intelligence says that the reds over there have been shipping hardcore rabble-rousers to London to influence and stir things up even more. Something's got to be done or we'll lose control over our own bloody city!"

"And am I to identify these Russians?" Lazarus asked.

"If you have the chance. But you are to report on all developments in socialist circles, Russians, Jews or anybody else."

Russians, thought Lazarus, remembering Katarina's pale breasts and the scent of her perfume, crumpled sheets smelling of their sweat in a Parisian hotel room.

Of course it was ludicrous to think that by coming into contact with some of her countrymen he would somehow be drawn closer to her. As the niece of a high-ranking member of the Okhrana, Katarina was no revolutionary. But for some reason, the mention of Russians made the whole business seem not altogether unappealing.

"Who is this fellow I'm to be working with?" he asked.